SOON

STORY RIVER BOOKS

Pat Conroy, Editor at Large

SOON

Stories

PAM DURBAN

The University of South Carolina Press

Published by the University of South Carolina Press
Columbia, South Carolina 29208

www.sc.edu/uscpress

Manufactured in the United States of America

24 23 22 21 20 19 18 17 16 15   10 9 8 7 6 5 4 3 2 1

Library of Congress Cataloging-in-Publication Data
can be foundat http://catalog.loc.gov/.

ISBN 978-1-61117-533-2 (cloth)
ISBN 978-1-61117-534-9 (ebook)

This book was printed on a recycled paper with
30 percent postconsumer waste content.

The stories in this collection were published, some in slightly different form, in the following publications: "Birth Mother," in *Atlanta Magazine;* "Gravity," in *The Georgia Review,* and reprinted in *New Stories from the South: The Year's Best 1997* and *Best of the South: From the Second Decade of New Stories from the South*; "Island," in *Five Points*; "Keep Talking," in *The Carolina Quarterly*; "Rowing to Darien," in *Five Points*, reprinted in *High Five: An Anthology of Fiction from 10 Years of Five Points;* "Rich," in *The Idaho Review*; "Soon," in *The Southern Review* and reprinted in *The Best American Short Stories 1997* and *The Best American Short Stories of the Century;* "Three Little Love Stories," and "The Jap Room," in *Shenandoah*; and "Hush," in *The Kenyon Review*.

CONTENTS

FOREWORD

In "Rowing to Darien," Pam Durban's first story in this collection, the title and theme of the collection—*Soon*—proves to signify more than a matter of easy closure or rapidly approaching time. The lone woman rowing desperately backward from Pierce Butler's plantation slavehold, forced to face what she is fleeing, watching a small place getting imperceptibly smaller under an enormous dark sky, is aiming toward a new life on the far shore. It may take all night. "So be it, she thinks, because once Butler Island is out of sight, she will be free." This is no house or field slave running away in a stolen skiff; this mere chattel drowning her past with each scoop of the oars is the Master's lady, Mrs. Butler herself, fleeing from her marriage, rowing for her life. In this paragraph is the first appearance in the book of one of Pam Durban's signature words: because. The clause may be subordinate, but the significance offers a clue to both the character's intentions and the author's method. Durban's authority and her believability come from her knowing why; she could simply state the fact, but it is important to her, and more subtly to our trust in her, that we will be taught why. The answer to any why—she reminds us again and again—is *because*.

A report of things made of facts and events can be as true as an encyclopedia or almanac. But a book made of facts and events *because* of other facts and events is a world with order, with time, luminous with meaning. Durban's use of because is rhetorical, personal, stylistic, philosophical; it sets the pace like a steady heartbeat. It justifies the forward motion of the stories: this by reason of that; this other due to the fact that . . . It is two-noted, like the human heart's own lub-dub. It is the subtext and ligature underlying her stately prose which is not dealt to us, like cards, but presented; her gift. Durban's use of because grants her stories their indemnifying dignity.

Life, in Durban's prose, is a series of turnings, transformations. Change is essential to the truth she tells about the mystery of life- as she wrote in her novel, *The Laughing Place*—"because the truth of any life is how it changes" and "everything is in its own small or large way a choice between life or death." She sets her stories of change strongly in place, in weather, in time, not to defeat change but because, as she explained to Valerie Frazier in an interview, "I was most interested in who people are and how they got to be that way, and what makes them or allows them to go on living in the face of everything that happens to them." Love is tested to its limits.

Consider the first lines in "The Jap Room," this collection's second story. "One morning in late October, the north wind blew, the sky lowered down over us like a flat gray ceiling and winter began . . . Every summer, a man plants soybeans there, and in the fall he plows them under. That week, he'd finished his plowing and now the crows and grackles wheeled over the field like clouds of ash blowing this way and that, quarreling over the leavings." Immediately, we are set in time and place, and we see that winter is "soon." Winter is about ash and leavings. Winter is not by schedule or calendar; it is the end of summer, the end of harvest, and the time of ploughing under, ash time, stubble, slim pickings, settling for. In this story, winter is not a time to look away, but to pay even more attention "because [they] still weren't finished with what needed to be done."

That brilliant natural note sets the tone for the entire collection, the process of "the endless motion of return" in the seasons of life, with the "warring truths" (as Martha, the character in "Soon" realizes) that "the trees had died, but the fruit would not fall." Martha discovers "hope could cling to nothing and a shriveled apple was all it took to bring love slinking back into this world. Inside the fruit she saw seeds; inside the seeds more fruit. In this motion she saw the turning shadow that eternity throws across the world and also the current that carries us there."

Pam Durban's acclaimed writing is always beautifully paced. The stories in this collection, *Soon*, have the beauty of that steadfast, noticing pace as well as the authority and mastery of both tone and overtones. There is the charm of sparkle, even twinkle, but the overall effect is of stateliness, equilibrium. Cello music, mellow music. September songs.

Durban has the authority and mastery of voice, of voices, to persuade us that these lives are true, their troubles and pleasures real enough to matter, to break our heart. We believe in these people, as she does. She here risks her own heart to engage ours. She is a master of her craft. Her themes and tone appreciate the price we must pay to ripen. There is humor here, but no malice. Wit but no victim of it. Rita Dove has written that "Grace is the hatchet's shadow on the green." Durban's characters do not always recognize that shadow for what it is; they struggle through the follies of youth and of age, unmended ways, fraying loyalties, second and third thoughts and after thoughts. Survivors of every type of human loss abound here, but especially the ones who think they are prepared. "Sure enough," the wife tells us in "The Jap Room." "I knew what would happen next." But we learn, as she does, that local certainty and habit are not the same as eternity on its roll, adding up and counting down.

Each story's characters face an individual challenge. From "Soon," this remarkable and simple declaration of a life's work and war: "What do you do with what you've been handed?" The loss-staggered protagonist in "Soon" is revealed as willing but not able: "She guessed that if you could just give up hope, your time on earth would be free of longing and its disfigurements. God knows she tried. But you couldn't."

Is soon a word of hope or of despair? We don't even start wondering until a voice from the grave-dark cave, as in "Hush" whispers, "Who do you think you are?" The character, a direly ill forty-something on medical leave, who had been a big man in his business world, for whom no one ever was late a second time, now hears in the word "late" an ironic mocking. He "needed to answer like a man who wanted to live."

Durban's autumn-themed and time-haunted portraits gathered into this collection have no rivals and few equals. Count her among great writers who focus on non-urban small-town "ordinary" lives. The ways people get lost and found and matter to each other, testing, honoring, betraying bonds and expectations, wising up, holding on, letting go with results and cycles and returns—these are generally the field of novelists who need and take a great deal more space and time to deliver their goods. Here, Pam Durban has created satisfying, deep, wide miracles of short stories. Celebrate them, not because I say so; taste and see: these are good goods.

Mary Hood

Rowing to Darien

March 1839, just after midnight on the Altamaha River. The air smells of silt and fish and wood smoke. The hoot of a horned owl carries across the water, the creak of oarlocks and the splash of oars. The moon is up, one night past full; it throws a bright track on the water, and across this track Frances Butler rows a boat with a lantern set on the thwart. Out under the big moon that lights the whole sky, the lantern flame looks like a fragment of the larger brightness escaping across the river. That's how she thinks of it as she rows—a mission, not a flight—to dignify the journey and keep the fear at bay.

Fear of the Altamaha to begin with. The river is wide and deep, and from the banks it looks slow, even sluggish, as it glides through the Georgia swamps. Go out onto it in a boat, and the story changes, for here at Butler Island, twenty miles inland, the river is still the ocean's instrument, the road the tides use to travel in and out of that country. On a tidal river, lacking strength and will, you go where the water goes, which is, it occurs to her now as she rows away from her husband's rice swamp, what Mr. Butler expected of her once they were married. He the river, and she the boat, carried on his tide. Whither thou goest; wives be subject to your husbands, and all the other trappings of this world in which she has found herself, down here in the dark pockets of his wealth, the flood and drain of his profitable estuary.

Now, as her husband's boatmen have taught her to do, she sweeps the oars back, dips them deep, pulls with all her strength, all of this done quickly, for in the pause between strokes, when the oars are lifted, the current grabs the boat and pulls it downriver. She is an accomplished horsewoman, a hiker in the Swiss Alps; she is no flower, but this is hard, almost desperate, work. The sleeves of her dress are pushed up over her elbows; her hair straggles out of its twist. She rows steadily away, but someone rowing a boat across a river has to face the shore she's leaving. One last trial, she thinks, and would have laughed if she'd had the breath for it: to be made to watch the scene of her downfall vanish, though in this endless flat landscape, that might take all night. So be it, she thinks, because once Butler Island is out of sight, she will be free. It is only a matter of time.

Back on Butler Island, the tall cane and the grasses stir and hiss. She sees the landing from which she'd launched her boat, then the rice dike and beyond it their house, then the kitchen house and rice mill and beyond the mill, a cluster of slave cabins. Smoke pours out of many chimneys there and flattens like a ceiling, so that the whole scene lies under a smoky haze lit by the bright moon. Otherwise, all is still. No torches move along the dike that separates the river from the rice fields; no light shines on the water, as it would if someone on shore held up a lantern and looked into the river. No one is searching for her yet. Across the Altamaha lies a wide marsh island, General's Island, and beyond that island, the town of Darien, a line of two-story warehouses and a dock from which she'll step onto a ship and sail away north, then home to England and become again the woman she was before she married Pierce Butler and came down to Georgia: mistress to no Negroes, no slaveholder's wife.

Seven years ago, she'd come to America with her father, the actor Charles Kemble, on a tour to raise money for the Covent Garden theater in London. The two of them performing scenes from *Hamlet, Romeo and Juliet, Much Ado About Nothing,* at theaters in New York, Philadelphia, Boston. The newspapers in those cities called her *glorious, sublime,* and everywhere they went people threw yellow roses onto the stage and shouted her name until she stepped out from behind the curtain to curtsy again and speak a few more lines.

Still, she found acting demeaning, a kind of drudgery, a nightmare, really, for a woman of her sensibilities. Waiting for her cue among the dusty drapes and props, the shabby backstage clutter. Then out onto the stages of those packed and stifling theaters where, in winter, tin stoves blazed in the aisles, and candles cast wavering shadows across the rows of upturned faces. She was a writer, a poet, a published diarist, sister in soul to Byron and Keats. Byron above all, that reckless hero poet-man of the tragic limp and swagger, whose poetry moved her, she once wrote, *like an evil potion taken into my blood.*

They had not been in America for long when an English friend, a fellow connoisseur of women, wrote to Pierce Butler at his home in Philadelphia:

You must go and see this Frances Kemble perform, he wrote. *Her eyes flash with passion, and when, as Juliet, she flings her head back in love's tormented ecstasy, you will be deeply stirred.*

The day after their first Philadelphia performance she walked into the outer room of their hotel suite to find Pierce Butler sitting down to tea with her father. He wore fawn colored trousers, a green coat and pale yellow satin vest over a creamy shirt. As she entered the room, he stood and bowed, then kissed her hand, held it tightly between both his own. His eyes were deep, soft, and brown; they'd flown to her when she'd walked into the room and stuck to her when she smoothed her hair, and when she spoke they watched her lips. "Please do sit down," she said. He wore three gold rings on one hand and carried a cane with a silver handle. He had a boy's brown curls, a small, moist, pouting mouth, a weak chin. He lounged when he sat, as though expecting to be served. In this luxurious room where yellow brocade swags and fringed drapes framed the tall windows, he seemed completely at home. "Miss Kemble," he said in his buttery voice, soft and broad of vowel, "I hope that in the future you will number me first on the list of your greatest admirers." He sat with his back to the window, sunlight pouring in over his shoulder.

She sat across from him, next to her father, in the circle they'd made with their chairs. "I might consent, Mr. Butler, had I such a list," she said, and then she smiled at him with her eyes as she sipped her tea. She set her cup back in its saucer. "Though in America I fear I shall be judged a traitor should I encourage such undemocratic ranking," she said.

"Then allow me to keep that traitor's ledger for you," he said. "I shall be honored to take the blame as fair exchange for being listed first in your favor."

She learned that he was rich, and that he would be richer when his father's last sister died and he claimed his share of the family's Georgia rice and cotton plantations. He was waiting for that day, passing time in a rich man's way: cards and music, the racetrack, the theater. Rich enough to follow her from Philadelphia to New York to Boston, to rent rooms in the hotels where she and her father stayed, to buy a front-row seat at every performance. He slid into her life that way and she let him come. First thing every night when she came out onto the stage, she skimmed the faces of the front-row patrons and there he was, smiling up at her, the silver handle of his cane shining. In New York, he filled her dressing room with yellow roses; in Boston, bottles of old Port and Madeira appeared backstage. In Philadelphia his carriage waited at the stage door to drive her to his house on Chestnut Street for a late supper. Once, she returned to her dressing room, exhausted after three curtain calls. Her face ached from smiling; her throat felt raspy raw; her legs ached from striding and curtsying. On the dressing table she found a pair of cream colored leather gloves tied up with a narrow, green ribbon, gloves so soft, so warm, they seemed to melt on her hands.

This went on for two years. The American tour. Flowers and port and gloves and candlelight. *Get this for Miss Kemble. Take that away. Quiet, please. Bring the carriage.* Mr. Butler the first on his feet when the curtain came down, leading the applause, pressing money into her father's hand. "For the theater," he would say, "for Covent Garden, Mr. Kemble." Riding in his carriage with the curtains drawn, falling into his arms. Deep kisses in the deep night, his words breathed into her ear: "Marry me, Fanny, marry me, marry me," until, resting in his arms, she began to feel the whole tiresome weight of herself, her vividness and intelligence, this life of roles and exile, and to imagine how it would be to shrug it off like a heavy coat and rest lightly, cherished, in his care.

So what has gone wrong, five years and two children later? Why is she fleeing without coat or bag across this dangerous river? In January, she and Mr. Butler had left their daughters, Sarah and Francis, in Philadelphia in the care of an Irish girl and traveled down to the Georgia coast. He'd come to inspect his properties and to oversee the rice planting at Butler Island and preparations for cotton planting at Hampton, a short distance down the coast on St. Simon's island. She had come for her own reasons.

On New Year's Day, they'd sailed from Darien to Butler Island on a sloop running up the Altamaha under full sail on the incoming tide. Sun a white disk in the palest blue sky she'd ever seen. The river had looked dark as strong tea and the winter marsh was a rippling palette of brown, red, gold, where flocks of red-winged blackbirds wheeled and settled in the grasses. After the pleated, rocky folds of New England, the landscape had looked startling: flat all the way to some dim, distant tree line or open to the horizon where the sky sealed itself to the edge of the land. A world of grass and water and sun, towers of clouds in the sky.

As the Butler Island landing came into sight, they'd stood at the rail together. He'd taken her hand, and feeling its warm pressure, she'd smiled up at him and renewed the private vow she'd made to rescue her husband's slaveholding soul from the darkness in which it now lived and kindle within it the light of moral conscience. From the pulpit of his Boston church, her friend and mentor Dr.

William Channing had often preached that it was the duty of every Christian opponent of slavery to accomplish this waking and kindling, for it was by this persuasive pressure of one soul upon another that slavery would be abolished, one slaveholder at a time. Sailing for Butler Island, she remembered how the light had poured in through the tall, clean windows as Dr. Channing preached and how she'd imagined Mr. Butler's soul bathed in that light, imagined it freed and rising to meet her own. She'd never loved her husband more than she did that morning, imagining his salvation as she sailed toward his rice swamp.

As the sails were furled and the sloop tied up at the Butler Island landing, the people swarmed out to them, weeping, dancing, clapping, crying *Massa* and *Missis,* kissing the hem of her dress, stroking her hair, until, frightened, she'd called out for Mr. Butler, who was laughing and shouting as he was plucked at, wept over. Up at the house, she found herself in a long, bare room furnished with a pine table and a sofa with a dull green baize cover where she sat for a long time after the noisy, happy mob had departed, one hand pressed to her chest to quiet her pounding heart. Candles flickered in sconces along the walls and on the table. At one end of the room, there was a fireplace, and as she waited for her heart to slow, he began to build a fire. When she found her voice again, she said, "This is idolatry, Pierce, or something very like it."

He knelt on the hearth, pushing sticks into the fireplace. "You are their mistress, now, Fannie," he said over his shoulder.

"I will not be worshipped," she said.

Already, he was weary of her intensity, her forceful mind. "Over time, you will acclimate yourself to their feeling for you," he said.

"I never shall," she said. "Not even if I live here for a thousand years."

It only *felt* like a thousand years since she'd come to this place. A thousand more to leave it. From her boat, their house on Butler Island looks peaceful. A whitewashed, square, wooden box of a house squatting on brick pillars behind the river dike. The rice fields begin behind the house and stretch for miles in every direction: from the house to the river and across the river and out of sight. In January the people had moved into the fields. They'd chopped and hoed the boggy ground; in late February, they'd sowed and tamped the rice seed. They opened the trunk gates and flooded the fields, squatted under trees at noon, scooping food out of cedar piggins with their fingers. Their children ran around half-naked, and when any of them got sick, they lay down on the floor of the sick house and recovered or died. Seeing them lying under their wretched scraps of cloth on the sick house floor she'd decided: if she must be their mistress, she would raise them up; she would teach them their worth. She went down to the slave settlements with lessons on cleanliness and order. She bought glass for the sick house windows, new blankets for the sufferers.

All winter, she went out in the long plantation canoe, up and down the Altamaha in any kind of weather. Primus, Quash, Hector, Ned and Frank rowed, and Kate's John, the foreman of the boat crew, rowed and shouted orders and led the singing that thrilled her to hear: wild songs on the wild water. She went out on horseback with Renty, Jack, and Ben moving ahead of her, hacking trails with their machetes through thick stands of oak and pine, through nets and loops of vines and creepers, and for these services (until he found out and forbade her to do it) she paid small wages to Mr. Butler's men, to teach them the value of their labor. That winter, from Darien to St. Simon's, their plantation neighbors talked: Pierce Butler could not control his wife, they said, that English actress, that scribbler, that abolitionist on a mission to their country, to her own husband, as though *he* were the one who needed saving. Every day, so they heard, every waking hour, she lectured him on the evils of slavery, on the will to power that corrupts master and slave alike.

A breeze comes up and cools her scalp and her face, which is hot with the work of rowing. She thinks of the flocks of swifts that skim the water in the daylight hours. She is one of them, she thinks, flying away. She thinks: you row and each stroke of the oars carries you farther from the place you're leaving. There is comfort in the simple, fact of distance and how it widens if only you keep moving in the direction you want to go. She's almost to General's Island now. Back on Butler Island, the dwelling house and kitchen house and the cabins behind the kitchen house look smaller, as though the distance were at last restoring order and scale, reducing Butler Island to a small place under an enormous sky. As she rows she sees one torch, two?—moving from the slave quarters toward the house. Perhaps the women are making their nightly pilgrimage to see her; it makes her smile to think of a dozen of them trooping in to sit in front of the fire. And only Pierce to listen to them now or to send them away.

Two weeks after they'd come to Butler Island, she'd invited the women to bring their needs to her, and every night they came to her as she sat writing at her table next to the fire at one end of the long, barnlike room. Nancy. Judy. Sophy. Sally. Charlotte. Sukey. House Molly. "How de, Missis," they said, and sat or squatted in front of the fire. They needed cloth they said, cloth and meat and cornmeal.

One night last week, she'd asked: "How many children have you had, House Molly?" thinking to record their histories in her journal so that one day the world could look into slavery's face, as she had done.

House Molly was a tall, thin, light brown woman with a long neck and golden eyes. She sat on the floor in front of the fireplace, legs straight out in front of her, massaging her knees. "Six, Missis. Four in the earth now," the woman said, staring into the fire.

She'd sat back in her chair, put down her pen. She thought of her own children in Philadelphia. She imagined them rolling hoops in the winter garden with the girl, Margaret, keeping a sharp eye on them. When someone asked about them, she did not find it necessary to say that they were still alive.

"Charlotte?" she asked the tall woman with the broad, flat, face who squatted next to House Molly.

"Three, Missis, all in the earth."

Sukey, who was short and very black, had borne four, though only two still walked the earth. A terrible mathematics. She covered pages with the sums and stories which they told in the plainest way. The women worked, they worked in the fields with the men, into the last weeks of pregnancy and went back to the fields three weeks after the children were born. Chopping weeds around the new rice shoots, up to their ankles in the gray muck of the fields, skirts tied up between their legs. Shoveling the rice field ditches in winter, out in the cold mud and the scouring wind. An occasional piece of fatty bacon or fish. Thin milk in their breasts, or none.

A dozen times a night her heart was broken by their stories, and she took their stories to Mr. Butler in hopes that his heart would be broken as well, for the chastened heart, the broken heart, is the heart that is ripe for salvation. But his heart would not be broken, it would not be touched. He lost the pages that she brought him; he folded and stuffed them in his pockets and never mentioned them again. He was planting a rice crop on Butler Island, cotton at Hampton. Surely his own wife could see that he was busy and not trouble him with the complaints of malingering women. Finally, last week, he'd forbidden her to bring him any more grievances. "You must no longer call me Missis," she said to them that night, after she'd told them that her husband would hear no more from her about their troubles. Who was this mistress they cried out to? She asked herself. Surely it was not she. She could not think of herself as mistress of this world in which children went into the earth and their mothers begged for help and she could not help them. House Molly had stood up then. "Night, Missis," she said, and the rest followed. "Night, Missis," they said, one by one, curtsying as they filed out. Now she is fleeing them, fleeing them all, their faces and their voices, the children in the earth. But their voices follow her as she rows, calling *Missis, Missis* across the water.

She has almost crossed the river now, and looking over her shoulder across General's Island, she sees the flickering light of candles in the upper story windows of the warehouses that line the Darien waterfront. She's that close. A short pull through the canal across General's Island that connects the Altamaha with the Darien River and she'll be there. She works one oar, then the other, steering toward the opening in the grass that marks the canal. As she rows she feels her heart lighten and lift. Soon, she thinks, soon she will break the river's hold and Butler Island will drop from sight as though it were a ship that sank, carrying her husband and his people to the bottom of the sea.

No sooner does she row into the canal than the bottom of the boat scrapes mud, the boat stops. It has taken her too long to cross the river and now the tide is dead low, the water all drained out of the canal. She knows the tide will turn; it will fill the canal and lift the boat, and on the other side of General's Island, the tide will sweep her up the Darien River, toward the town. But for now, there is nothing to do but pull in the oars and wait for the tide. Her dress is soaked halfway up the skirt and drapes heavily across her legs. She is tired and cold, and her heart pounds, her arms tremble from the rowing. Worst of all, the lighted windows and the chimney smoke of Butler Island still hang above the horizon, and she can still see the glow of a fire inside the kitchen house, which is where this desperate flight began.

Tonight she'd been sewing in front of the fire when Mr. Butler came in, dressed in a clean white shirt, his hair damp and combed back from his face. He'd poked up the fire then leaned over her shoulder, testing the cloth between finger and thumb.

"Fanny," he'd said, "oh, Fanny," in the fond, punctilious and lordly voice she'd come to detest. "On whose behalf are you straining your eyes and laboring over this cloth?"

She'd stabbed the needle through the cloth, pulled another stitch tight, tight. "For Judy, your cook, Mr. Butler," she'd answered, "who is in need of these trousers to ease the pain in her knees." In the fire, a log collapsed in a shower of sparks. She heard his breathing, she felt his hands tighten on the back of her chair.

"But what you must see by now, Fanny, is that there is no need for you to do this work when there are women always within the reach of your voice who will sew if you tell them to sew. For as I have told you many times, they are to us as these fingers are to my hand." As he spoke, he held out his hand to her, the simple junctures of wrist, palm, fingers illustrating the relationship he wished her to understand.

"They will never be the fingers of any hand of mine, Mr. Butler," she said, head bowed over her sewing.

Words had flown between them then about Judy's flannel trousers, then hotter words about the fact that his own wife felt free to match words with him at all. And during a pause in the shouting, she'd sewed the last stitch and bitten the thread, she'd stalked out of the house to find Judy.

The moon had risen then, fat and white, and smoke from the kitchen house chimney feathered out on the breeze. Just over the dike, she heard the river sweep by, its eternal windy rush, and from the kitchen house she heard Judy singing, a sharp, wailing song that slid up and down a mournful scale. She'd walked toward the sound. Outside the kitchen house door, in a wooden tub, she saw the hooves, legs and head of a sheep, dead eyes staring up into the sky. She stopped for a moment, stood on the round, flat stone outside the door and looked in. In the middle of the room, in front of the fire, Judy stood behind the chopping block, knife in hand. At the sight of Judy's bowed head, the sound of her voice, Frances Butler's heart grew quiet. She had come with the soothing garment; knowing her fondness for mutton, Judy was cutting up a sheep. She had never felt it before, the exchange by which her husband swore they all lived here: kindness or a favor given, work and gratitude returned. She smoothed the trousers, and Judy looked up, beckoned her with the knife: "Oh, Missis, come for see."

She stepped up into the kitchen house, into the smoky heat, the reek of blood, the thick, familiar smell of mutton. As always, the smell brought a picture to mind: sheep grazing on green hills under old castle walls, the tinkle of bells. England. The trencher on the corner of the wooden block was stacked with meat. "Look, Missis," Judy said, and she put down the knife and wiped her hands on her apron, "I be for cut the beautifullest mutton you ever see." Smiling, she held the trencher up to Frances Butler's face. She was a tall, stooped woman with a long, puckered welt across her forehead where the iron arm that held pots over the fire had swung out and burned her.

"Oh, Judy, thank you," she said. Then she looked down. The platter was stacked with strips, ragged diamonds, thick squares of bloody meat. Twice, three times, she'd showed Judy how to cut a sheep into proper pieces. She and Mr. Butler had laughed about the first platter of bizarre shapes that had come to their table; the second time, only Mr. Butler had laughed while Judy smiled and smiled and curtsied as though she'd handed Frances a plate of gold. She'd repeated the lesson a third time, tracing for Judy with a carving knife on a sheep's body the shapes of brisket, saddle, leg and joint. Three lessons and now the meat still looked as if it had been ripped from the sheep by a wild animal and spat onto the platter.

"Oh, Judy, now you really must tell me why it's so difficult for you to cut up a simple sheep," she said. Her voice came out sharper than she'd intended, and she saw in Judy's eyes a moment's cringing fear.

"Oh, Missis," she said quickly, twisting her hands in her apron. "I so sorry."

"Look at me," she said to Judy's bowed head. "I said look at me." The woman raised her head; the fear had cooled now, changed to something more watchful. She must be gentle, have patience. "You spoiled this meat again, Judy," she said, and then she stopped and waited.

Outside, the marshes croaked and sang; inside, the fire crackled. Judy watched the floor, pushed at the dirt with a bare toe. "Sorry, Missis," she said, again, flapping a rag at flies that had begun to settle on the meat.

As soon as she heard it, she knew it wasn't true. The tone was wrong, there was something quick and heedless about it, as if Judy had simply recited something learned by rote. It meant nothing. Now she would have to wait. If she'd learned anything in her time in this place, it was patience with these poor, wretched people who sometimes required many lessons to learn the simplest task. She would wait, and when Judy was truly sorry, she would forgive her, and then it would be finished and they would go on. That was all she wanted; it was little enough to ask and when enough time and silence had passed, Judy would realize that and give her what she wanted. And so she waited, and the longer she waited the more she wanted what she was waiting for until it began to seem that the apology she wanted belonged to her, and Judy had stolen it.

But Judy did not speak; the mutton lay on the trencher. As the silence went on, she thought of the respect that was being withheld from her, kept from her willfully, cunningly, with a great dumb show of humility, and she found herself studying the tools that hung on the kitchen house walls—the pokers and the heavy tongs. It seemed that she could feel the weight of each one in her hand, feel it brought down hard to break this unrepentant silence. That is when she'd dropped the trousers and run, climbed into the boat, lit the lantern and started rowing, each stroke carrying her away, away from Pierce Butler and from the rice fields and the kitchen house and the sorry-making weight of those tools that hung so close at hand. That is what she remembers from her perch in the mud of General's Island with the night almost gone and Butler Island still in sight.

Next morning in Darien she will find no northbound ship, no ship expected for days. She will be hungry and stiff and so tired all she wants to do is to curl up and sleep in the sun on the wharf among the bales of cotton and barrels of rice. The white men who pass her, sitting at the edge of the wharf on a trunk, staring into the river, will touch their hat brims and turn away. The black people will not look at her at all. "Missis," they will say and slip past her, heads down. Pierce Butler's wife. Before noon, the long plantation canoe will arrive and the six oarsmen will row her silently back to Butler Island, with her own boat tied behind.

Their separation will be long and bitter. She will leave him, and he will take her children, sell her favorite horse, Forrester, to a livery stable so that she will have to go back onstage to make the money to rescue him. They will try a few times to live together again and each time, before she moves back into Mr. Butler's house, his lawyers will draw up agreements for her to sign. *I will observe an entire abstinence from all references to the past, neither will I mention to any person any circumstances which may occur in Mr. Butler's house or family. I will not keep up an acquaintance with any person of whom Mr. Butler may disapprove.* Their divorce will be famous, the details printed in the Philadelphia newspapers. She will threaten scandal and he will swear she knows no names, has returned all the letters she's found. He will publish a statement in the Philadelphia paper offering evidence of her irrational anger, her refusal to yield to him, all the refusals that had doomed their marriage.

Still later, in 1859, after Pierce Butler has gambled and speculated away most of his fortune, the Butler Island people will all be sold. *The weeping time,* they will call it. A three day auction in a steady rain at the race track in Savannah. Pierce Butler will walk among his people there, carrying two canvas bags of twenty-five cent pieces fresh from the mint, handing out to each of them a dollar's worth of new coins.

So the details will be reported in *The New York Tribune.* By then she will be Frances Kemble again, alone with her newspaper on the porch of her house in Lenox, Massachusetts. Her American home, "The Perch," where her girls spend their summers and Emerson comes to call. It will be a bright, cool morning in May; the air smells of cedar and balsam. Goldfinches everywhere in the purple thistles. Down a long meadow in front of her house and through a gap between two low hills, a lake will shine in the sun. She will read the story three times, then drop the paper in her lap and close her eyes. And what she will feel then will follow her for the rest of her life.

Not the sorrow. She's ready for the sorrow; it sweeps through her like the tide in that long-ago river whenever she remembers the faces of House Molly, and Renty, and Quash, or Kate's John, or when she thinks of the children, the women who bore them and wrapped them in scraps of cloth and carried them to their graves. When the sorrow comes, she lets it carry her. She welcomes the sorrow, because by it she knows that the light of her conscience has not been extinguished. What catches her by surprise and holds her is the satisfaction she feels, like the kind that comes when some hard work is finally done, at the thought of Judy the cook standing humbly in the rain, holding out her hand for Mr. Butler's coins.

The Jap Room

One morning in late October fall ended, and in the twinkling of an eye winter was upon us again. I was hanging our clothes on the line behind the house when it happened. Out past the clothesline, the grass stops and a field begins. Every summer, a man plants soybeans there, and in the fall he plows them under. That week, he'd finished plowing and now the crows and grackles squabbled over the leavings. The overturned earth and the quarreling birds were the first sign. Then the sky came down like a low gray ceiling, the wind picked up and blew cold against me and winter had begun. Though the cold comes to this part of Ohio in the same way almost every year, I never have gotten used to the suddenness of it.

I could have stood there longer, watching the world roll along, but I felt Victor watching from the house, getting antsy for me to come back inside and see about him. Sure enough, there he was at the kitchen table, jiggling his knee and turning his lighter over and over in his hand, same as I'd found him every morning since he'd stopped working. Not that he could bring himself to tell people what he'd done; he acted like he was ashamed of himself for doing what every man deserves to do before it's too late to enjoy the time that's left to him.

For three months, I'd been answering the phone, and when Vic's old customers called, wanting him to tack up their gutters or lay a new roof over their heads, I spoke for him. "He's retired," I said, and he winced every time he heard it. Now, he looked at me out of those eyes that were as blue as faded cloth in the rough old map of a face that I knew every mile of. As a baby, Chicken Pox had marked him. In the war, he'd been shot through the face by a Jap sniper on the island of Luzon. The Jap bullet had knocked out some teeth, nicked his cheekbones and left a puckered scar on each cheek. "Let's have the weather report,

13

old lady?" he said. He counted on me for things like that: weather reports, storm warnings, predictions well or ill. When he smiled, his new teeth looked very white.

I set down my empty basket like I meant it. "That's it," I said. "I'm done hanging out clothes till spring." He jumped right up from the table and rubbed his hands. "Well then," he said. "I'd best get the clothes dryer fired up." He hunted up his tool kit and went to work, and before long I heard him whistling and banging away out in the laundry room, happy as you please.

Busy, always busy, that was my Vic, and lost without a job to do. We had our own brick home sweet home, bought right after the war. The banks loved a GI then. They'd give you almost anything. In my daddy's house, we hung our clothes on nails. Clothes on nails in the dark board walls. A bare light bulb in every ceiling. That's how I came up. When Vic and I married we bought a chifferobe. I'd never had a closet, and so, on the morning we moved into our new house, I opened all the closet doors, slid the kitchen drawers in and out. The windows fit tight and snug in their frames. They ran up and down just as smooth.

Now it was almost forty years later, and everything was still as tight and solid as it had always been; my Vic kept it that way. He said it was important to hold the line against rot or thieves in the night. Already he'd touched up the nicks in the white paint on the rocking chairs we kept on our front stoop and carried them out to the shed till next spring. He'd checked the furnace, ordered the fuel oil, put up the storm windows. He'd broken down his hunting rifle on the kitchen table, cleaned and oiled it and put it back together. Every time I saw the pieces of that gun spread all over the newspaper he'd put down on the table, I wondered how he remembered where they all went, but he said some things you never forget. When deer season opened in early December, him and his war buddies went hunting every day. The season was short and his gun had to be ready, and so did he. Every morning of deer season, he got up way before daylight, so he could be dressed and watching from the front window when they came for him.

I met Victor when we were both eighteen, in the fall of 1941, right before the Japs bombed Pearl Harbor. In the night, there'd been a cave-in over at the Eclipse Mine, and when morning came, I was there with Mama and my sister Emma, waiting for Daddy to come out or for someone to bring news of him. The dark was thinning into the gray light of dawn when the first of the men who'd been working the seam that caught the front edge of the cave-in started coming out by twos and threes, some walking, some leaning on others, and their families rushed up to meet them. Vic was in one of those groups, but nobody ran up to him. His people lived across the river in West Virginia, and word traveled slowly around here then: almost nobody had a telephone.

That was the first notice I took of Victor, the way he walked up out of the shaft like he was coming off his shift on an ordinary day, not expecting anybody to be waiting for him, not needing them to be, either. There was blood on his face, and as he walked out of the dark, he spat blood on the ground and looked at us like blood wasn't nothing, and he dared anyone to tell him it was. It was autumn then, too, the trees all on fire, and a maple tree on top of the mine entrance shone like pure gold when the morning sun found it. I pushed to the front of the crowd that gathered around Victor and waited to hear the news. He told us where the ceiling had caved in, said he'd heard picks behind the rubble. Men were alive there, he didn't know who or how many. The whole time he talked he looked at me, and I looked back, and I felt a bright confusion inside, like when the wind picks up red, orange and gold leaves and whirls them around together.

Later that morning, they carried my daddy out. His face was black with coal dust and deathly pale where the skin showed through, and his pants were torn and bloody. The bone stuck up from his leg in two places, but he was alive. By then, I was sitting on the ground next to Vic, with my hands balled up in the pockets of my sweater and the warmth of him warming me where our bodies touched. And that's where I stayed. I didn't get up and run to my daddy the way Mama and Emma did.

I have puzzled over that moment and puzzled over that moment, and even now, I couldn't tell you exactly what held me there except to say that once I'd found my way to Vic's side, I was home. Forsaking all others, I clung to him. There was something calm and sure about him, like he knew where he was headed and why, the way he'd looked on the morning of the cave-in: putting one foot in front of the other, walking out of the dark. I sat beside Vic on the ground. That night and every night after, I'd sneak away from my daddy's house and lie down with Vic on the damp leaves in the cool woods behind the bunkhouse where he lived with the other bachelors. Three weeks after that morning, we married in the courthouse over in Athens.

Now, my daddy was hot tempered and quick to judge, and he'd taken a dislike to Victor over something he knew, or claimed to know, about him. He said if I married Vic I was dead to my family. In those times, it was understood that a man wrote the laws that his family lived by, so neither my mother nor my sister came to hear us speak our vows, and from that day forward Victor and Wanda Pomeroy went on together, not asking for anybody's nod or blessing.

After supper on the night of the day when winter commenced, he went into the living room, and when I heard him pacing the floor, I knew what came next. Sure enough, before long, he slipped up behind me where I stood at the sink washing our dishes and rubbed my arms like he was trying to warm me up. "Guess I'll go on over to the VFW," he said. "You be OK here all by your lonesome?"

He said it like going to the VFW was a new idea. He'd been going to the VFW every Friday night since he came back from the war. Back in 1946, it was three rooms in the old company store building over in the Eclipse Mine town. When the mine shut down for good in 1950 and the VFW moved out to Chauncey, he kept on going, and now, even though he wasn't going anywhere dangerous or leaving me in danger, it seemed to ease his mind to hear that I'd be all right, so I nodded and I let myself rest against him. He wrapped his arms around me and rested his chin on my head and we swayed together like that, the way we always did when we said goodbye. Then he put on his jacket and his Cincinnati Reds baseball cap and stood by the kitchen door with his Zippo out, tapping a cigarette against it and waiting, because we still weren't finished with what needed to be done.

"Baby, I'm fine," I said. "You go on now, and don't worry about me. I'm going to take my shower and put on my housecoat and sit right here until bedtime." I walked into the living room and patted the seat of one of the corduroy recliners that our son Jasper and his wife Lynn gave us for Christmas last year—blue for Vic, green for me. "I'm going to sit in my chair and drink me a beer and brush my hair," I said. "Then I'm going to bed." He knew all about my routine, but he never tired of hearing about it, so I was willing.

"You go on, I'll see you later," I said this night, as always. Then, because he waited, hand on the doorknob, I said, "Come on home to me." I couldn't get distracted or leave out any part of it, or Vic would get worried. That Friday night, like he always did when I said that last part, he was satisfied. "Will do," he said, and he gave a little salute and out the door he went. Before he was even off the front stoop, the Zippo clinked open and I heard the lighter rasp, the way it happened every Friday night.

Come on home to me were the last words I spoke to him on that dread morning in 1942 when he boarded the bus with the other men from around here and went off across the world to fight the Japanese. Every day I put those words at the end of the letter I wrote him. He counted on those letters, he said, but he didn't write many of his own, just a few lines every now and then, half of them blacked out, all ending with the words, *Take care of yourself now, you hear me,* underlined so hard the paper was torn sometimes.

Now, I listened until the sound of Vic's car faded away up the road, then I sat down and started to brush my hair with one hand and smooth it with the other, and the feel of it carried me back to when it was long and black and cold against my hand, the way it was when Vic was overseas and I joined the Holiness Church. The teaching there was that the longer a woman's hair was, the more pleasing she was to the Lord, and I wanted the Lord to be so pleased with me that he'd have to let Vic come home, so for three whole years I let it grow.

Our church was what you call *Full Gospel,* and the gifts of the Holy Spirit, from tongues to prophecy, were alive there. Every Wednesday night and every Sunday morning during that war, I lifted up my hands, and the Holy Spirit came down like lightning and lit a path in my mind for Vic to follow home from the dark and shadowy places where he was in mortal danger. For a while after he came back, I kept going to church, but the storm had passed and the lightning was gone from the land, and finally I cut my hair and I was done with church religion.

I guess I thought he'd leave the war behind the way I'd left the church, or the way a black snake crawls out of its skin in the spring and leaves that whole, scaly suit lying empty on the ground, but when he came home, his skin was yellow from the malaria he'd caught in the Philippines, and you couldn't look far into his eyes without hitting rock. And skinny! He looked like somebody had cut a notch out of his middle. And of course there were the puckered scars on his cheeks where the Jap bullet had passed through and the smell of the hospital still in his shirt, and the first thing he did was he grabbed me by the arm like he was mad at me. "You been doing like I asked you to do?" he said. I matched his hard gaze with my own. "You're hurting me, Vic," I said. He let go right quick then, like he was surprised to hear it, and that's the last time he ever grabbed me, in anger anyway is what I mean.

Once when I was in my seventh month with Jasper, we were strolling down the sidewalk in Nelsonville when a jackhammer set in rat-a-tat-tatting. Well, Vic hit the ground and started crawling, dragging himself by his elbows.

I walked along next to him calling, "Victor. Hey, Vic, Vic," grinning at the people who gaped at us so they'd think we were playing. It didn't take more than ten seconds before Vic hopped back up and shook his head and brushed himself off, but that was the first time I saw how deep that war had sent its roots down into him.

And the tree that sprouted from those roots just kept getting taller and spreading wider. For close to forty years, he'd go to any school in the county that needed a man to talk to the children about the war. He was always a big hit, with his scars and his medals and his stories. He'd wear his uniform with the Silver Star and the Purple Heart pinned to it, and he'd tell the children how he'd won that silver medal by risking his life to get all his men off a landing craft and onto the island of Luzon without getting their asses shot off. He'd say that about their asses every time, too; no teacher was going to tell him to tone it down. The way he saw it, he'd earned the right to say anything he damn pleased about that war. It was his story, and he was going to tell it the way it had happened to him.

He'd tell the kids how the Japs charged at them with swords, and how his rifle company mowed them down like grass before the sickle and how a Jap sniper hidden high in a coconut tree nailed him, which is how he came by the Purple Heart pinned next to the Silver Star. He was alive, he'd say, because no Jap could shoot worth a damn. But American soldiers could, and before his blood had soaked into the Luzon sand, his buddies had hosed the Jap out of that tree and shot him a few more times just to make sure he was dead.

Vic was still mending in the hospital in Australia when the first bomb dropped, but by the time the second one fell, he was back with his men, and God bless Harry Truman and the atom bomb, and don't let the peaceniks tell you boys and girls anything different, he'd say. Then he'd snap to attention and salute them and he'd teach them how to salute back. I thought about those children while I brushed my hair. I wondered what they made of Vic's stories, what lessons they might have carried from them into their own lives.

It was after midnight when I went to bed. I turned out the light and lay in the dark, feeling grateful that there hadn't been a dance at the VFW tonight. I felt disloyal to think it, but there it was. It's a good thing other people can't read our thoughts and we can sometimes tell ourselves the truth—or as close as we can get to it—about the way things are for us without worrying about how our feelings will hurt somebody else.

The truth was, I was glad I hadn't had to drive to the beauty parlor in Nelsonville to get my hair yanked up into the French twist that Victor liked. I hadn't had to haul on the girdle and wiggle into his favorite red dress, or jam my feet into those high-heeled shoes that pinched and tortured so, or find myself at a table on the edge of the dance floor in that cold drafty hall, waiting with the other wives for our men to finish drinking and take us home. We'd have our shoes off, our girdles stuffed in our pocketbooks. The paper tablecloth would be soggy and covered with crumpled napkins and those little colored plastic swords that hold the cherries for the whiskey sours. Sometimes one of us would bring a deck of cards, and we'd play blackjack or pass around pictures of our grandbabies. Maybe we'd be a little tipsy, too, sometimes more. Mostly though, we'd just sit there and watch our husbands who'd forgotten all about us and congregated over by the bar, passing a bottle and drinking.

While they drank, our men were mostly silent, like they were just doing their jobs, the way they'd once worked in the mine, the way they must have done in the war together. Now and then, one of them would yell out a word that we couldn't make out, or say, "Hell, no," in answer to a question that nobody had asked, and someone would offer that man the bottle, and then they would all go back to watching each other drink. That was how it went now that we were older.

When we were younger, just after the war, we'd all get to drinking and dancing and whooping it up, and sometimes things got out of hand. This was when the VFW was up on the third floor of the company store in the Eclipse Mine town. The men would throw glasses and stomp the tables flat and light fires in wastebaskets. Now that I thought of it, I was surprised we didn't burn that building down, and ourselves along with it, and leave our orphaned children with a terrible story to tell about how their daddies and mamas burned themselves to cinders and left them to make their way through life as best they could.

One night the racket got so loud, the sheriff himself came out. Just him, no deputy. He climbed the steps up to the third floor, and Victor met him at the door. The sheriff was a stiff little red-faced man, packed into his uniform like a sausage in a casing, and when I saw him at the door, I said to myself, "Uh-oh, here comes trouble." Vic and the others bore him a war grudge for finding a way to stay home in Athens county while others went off to fight and die, and as I was beginning to figure out, no chain saw on earth could fell the tree that sprang from the roots the war sent down into our men. Words flew back and forth between Victor and the sheriff, and it got hot. Finally, something the sheriff said crawled all over Vic. He sprang, and in the blink of an eye, the sheriff's gun was in Victor's hand, and he was marching that lawman down the steps with me following close behind.

He called me his *second in command.* I was his *eagle,* because of my looks, and the war. Whenever you've got a war, you've got an eagle screaming down, with beak and claw, with murder in its eyes, to kill the evildoers and make the world safe for freedom. I had dark brown eyes and high cheekbones. I had a hair-trigger temper. Shawnee somewhere back down the line of my daddy's people, so I'm told. That night, Vic handed me the gun and told me to watch the sheriff while him and his buddies piled into the sheriff's car and turned on the siren and drove around the parking lot as fast as they could go, with gravel spewing up behind the car and dust smoking in the headlights.

Now, that gun was empty. I'll swear to that fact on a stack of Bibles. I'd watched Vic knock the bullets out and slip them into his pocket when the sheriff wasn't looking, but at the trial the lawman testified that I'd pointed a loaded gun at him, and the other wives were too scared to speak up for me. And I couldn't just say me and Vic were joking around, because it seemed wrong to make light of a man's fears for his life. I'd stood there in my bare feet with that empty gun poked into the sheriff's back, and he began to tremble and plead with me in a voice that never rose above a whisper. "Please, please," that's all he said, just those two words, over and over, but I knew what he was pleading for. I knew it was exactly what I'd be pleading for if it was me doing the begging, and I wanted to tell him the gun was empty, but I'd learned that you couldn't be on but one side of any fight, and I was on Vic's, so I shoved that barrel hard against his backbone and told him to shut up.

Vic got thirty days in jail for that stunt, and they might have sent me away, too, and put Jasper in the county orphan's home to boot if the Holiness church minister hadn't spoken up for me. The whole time Vic was in jail, I kept my head down and looked after Jasper and cooked for the men in the bunkhouse, and though my mother had not spoken to me since Vic and I married, she helped me through that time. Because in the same way it was understood that a man's family lived by his laws, it was also understood that hidden paths around the bedrock of his decrees could be found, and so, during those thirty days, food and money or scrip made its way from my mother to me. Even my righteous sister Emma chipped in. She wasn't but fifteen when she'd strapped on the full armor of God and took up the never-ending fight against Satan and his legions, of which, in her eyes, I was one. Emma would walk past my house with her head held high, looking neither left nor right, hair a shining river down her back, and later, on the porch, I'd find a bag of beans or a piece of salt pork wrapped in a clean dish towel.

Not long after Daddy died, Mama came to see me, and for the rest of her life, we felt our way back toward one another. I was the one holding her hand when she passed. My face was the last one she saw. But Emma went on her righteous way, and over time, the sin I'd committed by defying my father spread like a stain of wickedness through my whole life until, in her mind, I was lost and damned. And so I remain to this day, for we have not spoken in close to fifty years. I know she's alive, and I heard that once, in a tent revival over on the river at Gallipolis, she prayed in tongues for my redemption.

I woke up at four, knowing that Victor was on his way home, and my mind ran out to meet him. A thread always did run between us, like a strand in a web. Whenever he touched it, it hummed all the way to me. Outside, the moon had gone down, and the sun had not yet risen; it was the cold, deep-blue bottom of the night, and the stars burned sharp and quiet overhead. And then, just like I knew I would, I heard a car slow and turn down the driveway. Lights swung across the bedroom wall, tires crunched over gravel. The engine of our old Cadillac rattled on for half a minute after he'd shut it off, then silence fell, and I knew he was sitting in the car, smoking a last cigarette before he came inside. He was swigging from the bottle of Listerine he kept in the glove box, not to hide the smell of the liquor and the cigarettes but so that when he kissed me, I wouldn't say "Pew, Victor, you stink," and push him away. He could not stand for me to push him away.

That night, he sat in the car for so long I went to the window twice, pulled back the curtain and looked out, satisfied myself with the glow of his cigarette. I knew what he was thinking because I'd watched him think it a thousand times. He was counting out the month's money, going over and over it. He could cover five sheets of paper with the same set of figures, trying to make them add up to a different total. He was fretting over Jasper; he was worrying about me, some little twinge or sag or a moment of weariness he'd noticed. When he finally came inside, it was getting light outside, and he was just a dark shape swaying at the foot of the bed and fumbling with his belt buckle. This is where I came in. "Where you been, Vic?" I said, the way I always did. I trusted Victor, and he knew that. It wasn't tail he was chasing when he went out on a Friday night. He was too old for that now, but even when we were young, I'd known, the way I knew when he was almost home, that he'd not lay a hand on another woman.

Every time, he seemed relieved, like he *needed* me to ask so he could say it. "Jap Room," he said, breathing hard through his nose, and I felt my heart startle and grow heavy because I knew I had my work cut out for me. The Jap Room was a special room, kind of a shrine I guess you'd call it, that Victor and his friends had made of a room at the VFW up on the top floor of the company store in the Eclipse Mine town. They'd painted the walls red and hung a few American flags there, along with pictures of the Ohio men who hadn't made it back from the war. They'd left the ceiling white, and on it they'd painted the Japanese flag, the red sun and the red rays stretching out to the four corners of the ceiling, and when they got drunk, they'd yell and stagger around the room, clutching onto each other. They'd break bottles and punch holes in the walls and lie on the floor and cuss that Jap flag.

One morning when Victor hadn't come home, I went up there and found him lying drunk on the floor with an arm flung over his eyes. I saw another man throw back his head and howl like a wolf. When the VFW moved out to the new building in Chauncey, Vic and his buddies didn't make a new Jap Room there. *Good riddance,* I thought, but at least once a month, they all went back to the room in the old building—they couldn't stay away—and those were the worst nights of all.

I swung my legs out from under the covers and sat on the edge of the bed, with a hand braced on each knee. He was out of his pants and shirt now; he'd moved on to fighting with his undershirt. Any minute he was going to get himself tangled up in it and need my help. The one thing that made him panic was getting his head caught in something. On the nights when he'd been to the Jap Room, he fought it harder. "Come here to me, Vic," I said, and I yanked his undershirt over his head right quick, laying bare his white chest and bony shoulders. "There you go," I said. And he felt his chest to prove me right. Lord, I did love that man's body. Thin as he was, you might think he was puny, so it was always a surprise to feel how solid he was. When we were young, I'd wrap my legs high up around his back so he could get himself into me, as deep as deep could be. I said, "You're out of it, Vic, look here," and I held up his undershirt so he could touch it. I felt his knuckles, and they were raw, same as they always were when he fought his way out of that room.

I pulled a clean white t-shirt over his head and helped him into bed, and then I talked to bring him back. "Who all was there?" I said.

"Larry," he said, with his arm over his eyes. "Percy, Walter, Ernest."

"All your buddies."

"Yep," he said, but he kept on drifting out, away from me.

"Was old Henry Hines there?"

That did the trick. He snorted and took his arm down from his face. "What I want to know is, what kind of man keeps coming around where he don't belong?" he said. He bore some grudge against Henry, all that little knot of war men did, and from what I could piece together, they felt that he shouldn't have come back from the war when someone else didn't, but he had, and he wasn't one of them and never would be. Even so, he slunk around the edges of their pack and though they snapped and snarled at him, he always came back. Puzzling over why a man might do such a thing, we fell asleep.

When I woke up, the sun was high, and Victor was gone from the bed. *How strange,* I thought. Victor always slept late after a night at the Jap Room. I found him on the back stoop, watching the ash-cloud of grackles blow around the field behind the house. I thought he was smoking until I got around to where I could see his face. He had a cigarette in his mouth, but his face looked pale and clammy, and he couldn't flip open his lighter because his hand trembled so. "I can't seem to catch my breath," he said, trying to smile, fumbling at the lighter. "Feels like I been on a ten-mile run."

For a week, my Victor lay nearly naked in the ICU over in the hospital in Athens, his body a forest of needles, tubes and wires. Whenever they'd let me go in, I sat beside his bed and held his hand and watched his chest rise and fall. The screens above the bed kept track of his vital signs while a nurse sat on a stool and watched the screens and wrote down what the lines were saying in a big notebook. Once, while she was changing out an IV bag, she told me that a bad heart attack was like a car wreck inside your body, all your vital organs—your heart, of course, and also your lungs, brain, kidneys—shocked and jarred so badly it took a long time for them to sort themselves out and get back to work, if they ever did. She was careful to say that, too. If they ever did.

"He's in there, though," the nurse said. "You can tell he's in there."

She meant Vic, still inside his body. I knew he was in there, too, because whenever I said, "Squeeze my hand. Vic, squeeze my hand if you hear me," he always squeezed back. They said that was a very good sign. I raised my voice so he could hear me talk about him. "He's strong," I told the nurse. "He's a fighter." Then I got close to his ear for a private word.

"Come on home to me," I said, and he squeezed my hand again.

Finally they got his heart settled down, his blood pressure holding steady. They slid the ventilator tube out of his throat, and he went on breathing. When they moved him from the ICU to the heart floor, I walked beside the gurney, holding his hand. "Halfway home, baby," I said, and he smiled with his eyes closed and squeezed my hand.

For another week, Jasper and I took turns sitting with him during the day and sleeping in his room at night while he lay pale and unmoving, except to turn his head away when we tried to feed him. Whenever I asked if that was a good sign or a bad sign, the doctors said there was nothing to do but to wait it out. Jasper sat in the chair beside his daddy's bed, then I sat in the chair and patted Vic's arm or read or crocheted booties for somebody's new grandbaby while Vic slept and woke and stared at a picture on the wall.

Ever since they'd brought him to that room the picture had been giving him ideas. It showed the front porch of a green house, the railings lined with flower boxes spilling over with red and orange and yellow nasturtiums. He'd stare at it for a half-hour or more, with his eyes squinted up and his brow furrowed, like he was trying to answer a deep and puzzling question. Finally, one week from the fateful morning when he was struck down, he spoke. "Get one of those for us up home," he said, and spent his day's allowance of breath saying it. I stroked his forehead and said we'd get us a flower box for sure, just as soon as he came home.

"Pretty,' Victor said the next day, and I went to his side, smoothed back his hair.

"What's pretty, baby?"

"Picture," he said.

The day after that, I was reading recipes in a two-year old *Family Circle* magazine that I'd picked up from the ICU waiting room. With all the money they charge you for lying around the hospital, you'd think they could afford some up-to-date magazines. I was studying a recipe for beef stew when Victor said, "Ah," like another idea had just dawned on him.

"What, baby?" I said, but I didn't look up. I knew he meant that picture, and it was the sound of my voice he'd be listening for anyway. How many times had he told me that the whole time he was down in those foxholes with the Japs trying to kill him, it was my voice that promised him he was coming home? But I was tired of talking about that picture, and then, I was just tired, like something inside me had sat down in the road. I felt the strength drain out of me until I was too weak to lift my head. I don't know how long I sat there when it began to seep into my mind that a sound that had filled the room had stopped, and before I looked up I brought myself to it by slow degrees.

He was staring at the picture and his mouth was open as though he was about to tell me about his new idea. "Vic?" I said. "Victor?" I jumped up from my chair, and the magazine spilled onto the floor. I touched the scars on his cheeks, felt his banged-up knuckles that hadn't healed from that last trip to the Jap Room. Then his name just kept coming out of me, like waves were pushing it. Like I could call him back, because we weren't done yet. I'd just taken a minute's rest, and in that minute, he was gone.

"Victor, Victor, Victor," I called, until a nurse came running to help me look for him, and while she looked, I told her what I knew. He was a brave man, I said. Wasn't he a brave man to slip away like that to spare me the pain of watching him go? And she patted my back and said yes, he surely must have been. And the whole time I felt like I was out on a distant star, looking down at myself and the nurses and doctors coming and going and Victor lying dead on the bed.

That night, at home, once the doorbell stopped ringing and I'd made Lynn and Jasper go home and see about their little girls and stacked all the casseroles in the refrigerator, I came back down to earth, and I lay down under a running river of memories. Every time I closed my eyes, they'd start. And the next night, too, and the night after that, the night before Vic's funeral. I felt the sheriff tremble with that empty gun against his back, and I saw baby Jasper and Vic, curled up asleep together on an Army blanket in the green grass behind our house. But wherever those memories carried me, they always circled back to that hospital room and the way I'd sat there heedlessly while Victor passed. "Ah," Vic said, and I couldn't lift my head; I was so weary.

But it wasn't just weariness. There had been pleasure in it, too, and that's what troubled me, the pleasure of sneaking off so I wouldn't have to talk about that window box or anything else that might bring Victor home once and for all. Ever since the war, it looked like he'd needed someplace to head for, and that place was me. Now I was the place he was never going to get to, and I sat there like a ghost.

Then I was back out on that star, watching myself hold tight to Jasper's hand and walk toward Vic's grave, my heels punching holes in the thick, green moss on the ground of the cemetery across the river in West Virginia where Vic's people are buried and cedars stand among the graves, as green as life eternal. It was fall again, and the maples and hickories were on fire, same as the day we met; the sky bright blue and swept clean of clouds as though by the wind our lives are forever striving after, or so the preacher in Ecclesiastes says. I felt like I was walking in a dream, and the honor guard and Jasper were in it, too. Walking with long pauses between steps, the strong, young soldiers carried my Victor from the hearse to the grave. They walked so slow, like they were moving through water, and the light flashed on their white gloves and their swords and the bright, new flag draped over Victor's casket.

I didn't go to church anymore, but Jasper did, and once we'd taken our seats, Jasper's preacher promised us that those who believe in Jesus will have eternal life. On and on he went in that vein. He talked about how we should rejoice because Vic had gone to heaven, and he smiled as he spoke, like he was setting a good example about how not to give in to something as trifling as sorrow. Then the honor guard fired their rifles three times, and a bugler played *Taps*. That's when Jasper laid his head on my shoulder and covered his face with one hand. I rested my cheek on his head. Victor's war buddies huddled up together and held a salute till the bugle's last notes trailed off. I looked at their dry, cracked old elbows and I didn't cry. No sir. Those last two days, I'd cried all the tears I could cry; what was left inside me felt as dry as corn shucks that rustle against their stalks in autumn when the passing wind stirs them.

The honor guard picked up the shell casings of the bullets they'd fired and folded them tightly into the flag. As they worked, their gloves flew like a flock of white birds. Then one young soldier went down on one knee in front of Larry Bolton and gave him the folded flag, like I'd asked them to do. I wanted Vic's war buddies to have it, to hang on the wall at the VFW in Chauncey. They could put Vic's picture there too, and get drunk and howl and drag him back into the fight again. The Silver Star I gave to Jasper, to help him remember his Daddy's bravery.

Finally, finally, it was over. I kissed and hugged all the old men, and told them I'd join them in Chauncey directly. I smelled whiskey on the breath of Henry Hines and on Larry Bolton, too, clutching his flag. I kissed Lynn and my grandbabies and sent them on their way. I would have sent Jasper, too, but he wouldn't leave my side. People got into their cars and drove away, but I stayed. Long ago, I'd promised Vic that I'd walk with him as far as I could go, and I meant to keep that promise.

After the undertaker's men filled the hole to the top, they got out their rakes and leveled and smoothed the soil. At the head of Vic's resting place, they set up the flag made of red, white and blue carnations that his war buddies had sent, with the words *At Ease* stamped in gold on the red ribbon stretched across it. When I was sure I'd kept my promise, I rose from my chair, but then my knees went weak, and I had to sit back down. Jasper sat down, too. He held my hand and spoke to me so sweet and kind, and still the pain rose in me until I thought I'd drown in it. Victor was gone, he was gone from this earth. I would nevermore see his face or hear his step, look into his eyes or feel his hands upon me. And what was worse, I was still here, and the world was still the world that I'd never made good enough for Vic to come home to.

So where do you go, what do you do, when there is nothing more to be done, and the world is bare and empty? I wasn't ready to go to Chauncey to be hugged and fussed over and made to look at pictures of Vic, grinning from a coconut tree in his sunglasses and skivvies. That's when I hit on the idea of going to the Jap Room at the company store over in the Eclipse Mine town, the way Vic had done so many nights of his life. I wanted to see if I could catch a glimpse of the Vic I knew. Spirits linger, I told myself. Voices snag in the net of the air. Even the dust echoes. I missed Victor so much, I would have walked down into hell itself to find him.

Jasper drove me there in the big, black Chevrolet pickup he bought a couple of months back, when they promoted him to manager at the Kroger over in Nelsonville. On the way, we talked about how much that truck had pleased his daddy. Right after he bought it, Jasper drove over and took us for a ride, and now my son and I talked about how Victor had fiddled with all the knobs and dials and how he'd rolled down the window and hung his head out and whooped when he heard that V-8 engine hum.

Jasper eased his truck down the rutted road into the Eclipse Mine town, past my daddy's house and the house where Victor and I first lived as man and wife. All the houses were locked and barred, lumber and concrete block stacked under blue tarps in the yards. A real estate man from over in Athens had bought the whole town, and he was fixing it up. I'd read about it in the paper. A railroad track used to run past the company store, but a few years back they'd torn up the tracks and paved over the railroad bed. It was a bicycle trail now, and the word going around was that the man who owned the town had plans to fix up the company store as a place where people riding the trail could stop for a moment's rest, a cool drink and a bite to eat, before continuing on their journey.

The company store was the same old, rambling, gloomy barn it had always been. Someone had padlocked the front door, tacked up a new No Trespassing sign, but we went around back, to another door I remembered. It was held shut by a feeble little lock that Jasper soon forced, using skills he'd carried over from his brief spell as a juvenile delinquent. We pushed the door open and went inside. Outside, it was high noon, but inside it was so dim we had to wait for a minute or two while our eyes got used to the dark. Then I took Jasper by the hand and led him to the stairs, and we started climbing.

On the third floor, a scrap of ragged curtain on a rusty rod blew in at a busted out window. In a piece of mirror nailed to the wall, I thought I saw my own young face, but I didn't look twice and push my luck. The door into the Jap Room had sagged on its hinges so I had to shove it open, and it scraped over broken glass as it moved. The color of the walls had dimmed from bright red to dull rose. I caught a whiff of stale sweat and whiskey. There was busted glass on the floor and dust over everything, and all those holes the men had punched in the walls.

"Where are we, Mama?" Jasper said.

"The Jap Room, " I said to hush him. I needed quiet to look for Victor. I worked my way around the walls, touching the holes, feeling of their ragged edges. When I come to Vic's, I told myself, I'll know it. But when I'd gone all the way around and felt of every hole, I still couldn't pick out Victor's from among the rest. And I felt again the pain of his going, and I was reminded of how I'd deserted him at the end and left him to pass on alone, so I said the only thing I knew for sure. "He is not here," I said out loud, and as soon as the words left my mouth, I knew that he was forever free from wandering the earth, trying to find his way home, and so I said it again. "He is not here."

Jasper mistook my joy for sorrow. He reached for my hand and squeezed it. "We'll always have him in our hearts, Mama," he said.

"Yes, we will," I said, and I squeezed back. And then he started talking about his daddy and how it comforted him to imagine Vic in heaven, fishing in the river that flows by the throne of God. I didn't believe in the fishing, the river or the throne, but I let him go on, because as I listened to him, it came to me that he was telling that story for the same reason I've told this one. There's what happens, and then there's what you make of what happens, the story you tell, so you can take it.

Three Little Love Stories

Riddle Me This

I felt safe in the car in front of Joe and Linda's house, with the sun rising and the dark shapes around the house turning into fences and pines. It was comforting to see things reliably turning into what they were. The unpaved street looked familiar, and I tried to remember why as I checked the rear-view mirror and watched for a light to come on in the house so I could go in and tell my friends what had happened and ask them to let me stay for a few days while I figured out what came next.

The husband I'd run away from that morning was some fraction Cherokee, tall and graceful and strong. We were just out of college when we met, though *met* is too humble a word for how we started. I need a bigger word to conjure that moment. Something tectonic, maybe, something momentous. Collided might work. Drowned. I was new in town and looking for a place to live. He lived on the grounds of a big, brick house that had once been a rich man's home. By the time we found one another, crabgrass traced every crack in the long, curved driveway; the lawn had surrendered to dandelions. The house itself was a warren of incense-soaked rooms with Jimi Hendrix, Janis Joplin and Rolling Stones posters on the walls. In the kitchen, a pot of brown rice always bubbled on the stove. He'd built himself a loft in the greenhouse, and when I walked in, he was perched on the edge of the platform, eating a slice of cantaloupe.

I looked up and he looked down and smiled, the juice ran down his chin, and when I picture that moment now, forty years past the fear and confusion, the rage and sorrow and regret that came later, what I remember is the startling joy of seeing his face for the first time. What I remember is how we tumbled, slid, flew into a bright maze of love.

I moved into his greenhouse that day, and when his grandmother heard we were living together, her blood pressure started climbing. She might have a stroke, his mother said, she might *die,* if we didn't stop living in sin and get married. Living in sin? we said. Married? The words tasted rancid and stale. Jimi, Janis and Mick had never used them. But the man I loved was her favorite grandchild, and so we went to see his grandmother. She lived in the country outside of Columbia, South Carolina, in a small white house under a big water oak, on the farm she'd worked with her husband since they'd married at fifteen.

"I feel like I already know you," I said to her through the screen door that she unlatched to let us into her kitchen. And that was true. Every night we lay in his greenhouse loft, under the clear night sky and under the rain, filling ourselves with each other's stories, adding them to our own. I knew about how his grandfather shinnied up a pecan tree one day to shake down the nuts, and the next day he dropped dead. I knew that every fall on hog-killing day, his grandmother led her daughters and nieces behind the barn to boil and scrape the intestines, to spare the men that awful stench. That detail had stuck with me: The women scraping hog guts behind the barn so as not to offend. But that world, like the world of living in sin, was already so far behind us the distance made it harmless. We could look back at it tenderly, excusing its faults and cruelties as though they'd happened in a dream.

"Well, come on in the house," she said, and unlatched the door. She shook my hand, refused a hug. My love and I sat next to each other and held hands under the table while she peeled apples in continuous spirals and sliced the fruit into a dishpan for the pies she was going to make later.

"We're married in our hearts," he said, but she kept peeling apples. I loved his earnestness then, and remembering it now, I still love it, and that feeling surprises me, the way remembering the moment we met surprises me. I thought even the memory of love had been smashed and lost, along with the love itself. And of course he didn't convince her we were special or exempt from any rules. When we left, she latched the screen-door behind us and walked back inside. That was a bad sign, he said later. At the end of a visit, she usually loaded him down with food and waved from the back stoop while he drove away. Sure enough, she went on fretting and grieving, grieving and fretting, and finally we gave in. We were already married in our hearts, we said, what difference did a few words and a piece of paper make?

We got married and moved down to Atlanta, where he went to work on a construction crew, building houses in the ever-expanding suburbs. Once I watched him carry a whole sheet of plywood across the roof beam of a three-story house and I was not afraid; he was that sure-footed. But before long, he was cheating on me and I was cheating on him, to get even. Cheating was what sent me to the street in front of Joe and Linda's house. The night before that dawning day, my husband had gone out, the way he did almost every night, and when he wasn't home by midnight, I walked across the street to the party I'd left earlier, and the host and I finished what we'd started. At five, when I went home, my husband was pacing in the yard. If an upstairs neighbor hadn't heard the shouting and come down to help, who knows what might have happened? But he did, and I got away and drove to Joe and Linda's place, and two days later, while I was hiding out there, my husband found the body of a woman who'd been stabbed to death and dumped in the kudzu on some vacant land near our house.

I read an article once about how the drive for revenge lights up the same part of the brain as hunger or thirst. Amen I say to that. I haven't seen or talked to my first husband in close to forty years, but whenever I remember the story of the murdered woman, I hope the police noticed his wedding ring and asked him where *his* wife was. And I hope when he realized he had no answer, he felt his capable self collapse into a small, threatened creature, the way I felt it happen to me on the morning he could have killed me. I wish that for him as sincerely as I sometimes wish him well. Even now it's satisfying to imagine the cops waiting for an answer, and him with no place in his mind where I could be found.

I must have slept for a few minutes in front of Joe and Linda's house, because when I opened my eyes again, the night was finished and a new day had begun. I saw the road with fresh eyes, too; I knew why it looked familiar. It was like the hard-packed dirt road in front of the house where I grew up, the road I used to walk out onto and imagine how far from home it could take me. Like the dirt road from my childhood, this one could carry me away, too, and that morning, I let myself follow it. I drove away from him and us, crossed a country's worth of rivers, mountains and deserts. I drove until I came to a place where the past was gone, and we had never met.

All Hallows Eve

When he opened the door to let her in, he was dressed for the costume party in a pair of wide brown trousers and beige suspenders, a white shirt with a pillow stuffed inside. "Who are you?" she said. They'd known each other six months.

"Myself a few years ago," he said. "This is my largest shirt, a size 20, my biggest pants, size 50." He'd lost a hundred pounds since he'd worn those clothes, and she was glad she hadn't met him when they fit. Wearing them again made him thoughtful. He held out the waistband of his old pants. "When you're fat," he said, "people treat you like you're not human. Who are you tonight?"

She unbuttoned her cloth coat to show him a pink shirtwaist dress with a wide skirt and a patent-leather belt. She was wearing high-heeled shoes, rhinestone ear clips. June Cleaver was the general impression she was going for, someone she'd never been. "Forget the party," he said. He took her hand and led her to the bedroom. She was an accomplished woman, but sometimes she liked to be bossed. He worried that he was too gentle, so bossing her suited him, too. Playing this game, they both felt free and new.

In the bedroom, he shed his fat man's clothes. "Come sit next to me," he said. "Don't take your clothes off until I tell you to." They went on like that until she was naked except for her bra, with one strap pulled off her shoulder, and a small gold locket that rested in the warm hollow of her throat. "Get up and put on some lipstick," he said. She did, and when she sat down on the bed again he touched the locket and pulled her down and kissed her, hard enough to insist but not to hurt—that was their understanding—but suddenly, she was afraid, and he saw that and stopped playing. "Tell me," he said.

Something that happened a long time ago, she said, when she was running from that first ruined marriage. She was spending the summer in London, sleeping on the floor of a friend's room over a pub and washing dishes in exchange for a place to stay. She drank too much in London, she slept with a lot of men because she believed back then that being reckless made her free. Even now, she told him, she remembered the thick smell of mutton fat from the scraps of shepherd's pie that she pushed off the greasy plates and into the slop hole in the kitchen at the pub.

There was one man in particular, she said. Irish. He came into the pub every afternoon with his morose longhaired friend who jumped up from his chair every time he saw her, stalked over to the jukebox and punched in "American Woman." One drunken night, the three of them went back to the Irish man's flat in Camden Town, and he got rough with her while his friend sat in a chair beside the bed and watched. She remembered the gritty sheets against her back, the smell of beer and dirty clothes, the way his friend watched and laughed. "Not human," she said. "I know how that feels." That night she'd been a piece of glass, a rock on the bottom of the ocean, far away from what was happening to her.

Her locket came off that night, she said, but she wasn't leaving without it, and after the friend left and the Irish man passed out, she found it in the tangled sheets. And then the sky was getting light and she was outside on the sidewalk in Camden Town, flagging down a taxi, holding the locket tightly in her hand. On the ride back to the West End she'd looked at it gratefully from time to time, as though it had saved her life.

"And here you are," he said, and he touched the necklace lightly.

"Here I am," she said. "Here you are." She moved her hands over his belly, which was all that was left of the fat man he'd been. They'd both come to this bed accompanied, hoping for welcome.

Little Bone

Now it is a cold, bright January day. She sits at her dining room table, eating a bowl of minestrone soup and watching the birds mob the feeder that the man she loves has hung outside the window. She's a long way from the dirt road at dawn, from London and the slow collapse of a second marriage. Best of all, she's done with the old-maid years. Years of virtuous thriftiness, when she used the same sheet of tin foil three times and rinsed out her sandwich bags and trained herself to expect nothing. Now this, she says to herself. Now this. Meaning the soup, the birds, the light pouring through the dining room window that warms her face the way the man warms her with his hands and his mouth. Meaning: this happiness. She's enjoying herself like that when she bites down on something hard.

Who put a stick in the soup? she thinks, but it's a little leg bone, the kind a witch might pull from her mouth when she was done with the little man she'd feasted on. The sight of the bone shocks her, like an insult in a pleasant conversation, and right after the shock comes the thought that she could have choked on this bone. She could have choked to *death*. Choking to death while eating alone is one of her most vivid fears. During the thrifty years, the idea of choking to death had come to stand for all the dangers of living alone, without love.

Next morning, she finds the bone on the cutting board beside the sink, where she left it. It's dry now, white as an ancient relic, and so light it feels almost harmless. Though of course it isn't harmless, and she knows that, too. She can as easily choke to death on a dry bone as a wet one; she can choke as easily now when she feels rich as when she felt thrifty and poor, and how is that fair? she'd like to know. But we're alone sometimes, aren't we? With love or without it, you drive or eat or walk or breathe alone. Your heart, of course, always beats alone. The dangers multiply as endlessly as the chances for happiness. Multiply and sprawl and mush together until it all looks like the same big chance called your life, the only chance you've got.

Later, as they sit outside together, watching night come down, she tells him about the bone in the soup and about her fear of choking to death alone. For this fear, as for others she has confided in him, he has a cure; he'll teach her how to do the Heimlich maneuver on herself against the back of a chair. "What if you're choking in an empty room? " she says. "What if you're choking outside without a chair in sight?"

She sees by his face that she's let him down again. In spite of his tenderness, his efforts to soften her hard places and heal her of pessimism and wariness, she's imagined the worst, again. "Why do you say things like that?" he asks, and she's sorry, sorry. She's not being flippant, but who knows what will become of them, of anyone? Any soup can have a bone in it, but maybe no one will choke, she says. Maybe the odds are in their favor.

He can live with that, he says. The *maybe* he means. The possibilities. She says so can she.

Gravity

Whenever she visited her mother in the last weeks of the old woman's long life, Louisa knew that if an aide had turned Mother's wheelchair to face the Cooper River she would be hearing the story about Mamie and the bridge again. On her mother's bad days, which seemed to fall at the beginning and end of the week, bracketing the lucid days, Mamie looked back at her out of the face of the nurse, the aide who brought her meals or helped her to the bathroom: if she was black, her name was Mamie.

Also, any footsteps might be hers. "Mamie?" Her mother's voice would wobble out to meet Louisa as she walked down the hall toward her room. "Mamie?" Mother would be watching the door, hands folded in her lap and a look of pained brightness on her face, until she saw her daughter and the brightness dimmed. On the good days, her mother laid down her search for the actual Mamie (dead, now, for fourteen years), and made do with Mamie's story. In the last weeks of her mother's life, Louisa thought of the Mamie story as a lighthouse beam: whenever the old woman sailed too far out of sight of land, she swung toward its light and traveled home.

Now it was the Friday before Palm Sunday. She'd been outside hanging the sign on the wrought-iron front gate before heading out to visit her mother when she'd heard a horse's hooves in the cobblestone street and the rumble of carriage wheels. "Kindly Admire the Garden from the Street," the sign read, green words painted on gray slate with flowering jasmine twined around them to sweeten the message: go away, no one here wants to talk to you about this house, its people, or its history. *Not a moment too soon,* she thought as she ducked behind the big tea olive beside the brick walkway, and the carriage stopped in front of her house.

As she waited in the tea olive's fragrant shade, she asked herself again: Why this obsession with Mamie? Surely her mother wasn't trying to decide where Mamie and her family had fit in their lives. Those issues had all been settled ages ago. *A good pair of black hands,* Mother still called Mamie, and sometimes the thought brought tears to her eyes. In her more formal moods, she called her *the laundress and housekeeper and cook.* Finally, when Mamie got too old to work, she became *the family retainer* who lived in the converted kitchen house at the back of their yard. How old was Mamie? No one knew. No white person anyway. "They destroyed my dates" was all Mamie would say if you asked her age, then set her jaw as if she'd clamped a plug of words between her back teeth.

"Who destroyed them, Mamie?" Lousia would ask.

"I be just born, time of the shake," she would say. At least that date was fixed by something other than an old colored woman's memory: the earthquake of 1886. Then would follow a long, tangled account of dates written in a family Bible that was burned up in a fire in some forgotten year. But in spite of a few misplaced dates, the longer history was clear.

Mamie's family had served the Hilliard family since time was, in slavery and in freedom, down through the generations, right up until the day when Mamie's sixteen year old granddaughter, Evelyn, left the kitchen house where her grandmother had raised her, went to live with relatives on John's Island and cut the two-hundred year-old ties that had bound the families together.

The tour guide was an affable, blond boy, recruited, no doubt, from the endless supply at the College of Charleston. He wore a gray Confederate army cap and a red, fringed sash around his waist. The carriage horse, a chestnut Percheron, dozed with one back hoof cocked on the pavement. The boy stood up in the front of the carriage and turned to face his passengers, the reins draped loosely over one hand. This much she could see. And what she could hear was the story she'd been hearing all her life. Even though she'd been born a Marion—her father's name and fine in its own way, with Francis Marion, the Swamp Fox, occupying the place of honor at the head of that ancestral table—she and her mother had always thought of themselves as Hilliards first.

The Hilliard house was one of the finest examples of a typical Charleston house still standing, the tour guide said. Set gable end to the street, with piazzas up and down and a garden tucked behind a brick wall, its architecture was West Indian. Specifically, its influences could be traced to Barbados, from which windward isle many of the planters had made their way to the Holy City of

Charleston. She flinched at the soft movie-mush of his accent that made him sound like the Southern aristocrat in a bad melodrama.

"Please note the exceptionally ornate ironwork of the gate," he said, "and the iron spikes set along the top of the brick wall as protection against the pirates who once roamed and pillaged through these streets. Notice the bricks of which the house and its garden wall are constructed," he said. "They were fired in the brickyard at Fairview, the Hilliard plantation out on the Edisto River."

Now, as was the custom with wealthy rice planters of their day," he said, bowing slightly, "the Hilliard family owned this house in town and the plantation house at Fairview, and they divided their time between these two residences. In late winter, they came into the city for the balls and races of the social season, then left for the plantation in time to oversee the planting of the rice crop in the spring. During the summer, the sickly season, they lived in town, then journeyed back to the plantation for the fall harvest and stayed there through the Christmas season."

Finally, it was over. The guide clucked to the horse and the carriage moved on, leaving a pile of golden droppings on the cobblestone street. Closing the iron gate behind her, Louisa stepped carefully over the slate flagstone sidewalk in front of this house where the Hilliards had lived forever. That spring Louisa was seventy-five, and her body felt rickety, full of drafts and cracks. Crossing the uneven flagstone sidewalk in front of her house, she felt her frail ankle bones, her brittle spine and rigid hips. Sometimes at night she imagined the calcium sifting out of her bones, as though her body were dissolving. Soon, she would look as old and rounded as a a tabby foundation after a few centuries out in the weather.

Still, thanks to a daily dose of estrogen and to willpower, she could still hold herself erect as she walked, a woman with a narrow, quiet face, a Prince Valiant helmet of white hair, wearing a raw silk, teal shirtwaist dress accented with a dramatic scarf. She carried a flowered portmanteau and walked with her head upright and quiet on a long neck, enjoying the subtle prickle of salt air on her face, the smells from the gardens she passed, the sound of trickling water, the cries of gulls. Passing the market and the wharves, she walked through the smells of fish, coffee, and incense. The ship's chandler's shop was open for business, and the hayfield smell of rope drifted out of the narrow door. In the harbor, the sheer green side of a freighter rose, the red and white Danish flag flying from its bridge.

At the private nursing home in the old house on Society Street where her mother lived now, Louisa tiptoed up the stairs and down the hall until she came to her mother's room. This was Friday, one of the bad days, and so her wheelchair faced the window and the bridges. "Mamie?' her mother asked, without turning around.

"It's Louisa, Mother—here we are," she said as she always said as though they'd arrived together at some destination. Her mother grunted and turned away, but she didn't let it bother her. She pulled a chair close to her mother's wheelchair, lifted her needlepoint out of her bag and went to work on the paschal lamb that she was stitching on the linen Easter banner for St. Phillip's Church. While her mother pouted, Louisa crossed her ankles, straightened her back, smoothed her face, willed her mind to become a quiet pool of forbearance.

Soon the heap of quilted, pink satin with the failing heart and lungs that Louisa called Mother began to stir. "The Cooper River Bridge was the bridge we had to cross, you see . . . " she said, eddying into the story's current. *Poor old soul,* Louisa thought, and an image came to her of something smooth and heavy, like an old marble egg. Maybe she told the story of Mamie and the bridge because it was the only story she remembered that could still carry her away from her present life. But what amazed Louisa, and sometimes made her want to jump up and scream, "Get to the point, for God's sake, Mother!" was how the story never varied from telling to telling by one detail, pause, or inflection; how it seemed to always ask a question at the beginning which was never answered by the end.

One morning in the reading room of the Charleston Library Society, as she searched a copy of the *Charleston City Gazette* from the summer of 1820 for a mention of some nineteenth-century Hilliard, Louisa came across this advertisement: "$10 Reward. Drifted from Haddrill's Point, a CANOE, painted red or bright Spanish brown, branded with my name in several places, has row locks for 6 oars." That is how she thought of her mother's mind: a one-hundred-and-two-year-old Spanish-brown canoe of a mind, drifting here, drifting there, stranded on an oyster bank at low tide, lifted and set adrift when the tide came in, drawn by tides and currents always back toward Mamie and the Cooper River Bridge.

"The Cooper River Bridge was the bridge we had to cross, you see, to get from the city over to our beach house on Sullivan's Island. We spent our summers there away from the city's heat," she confided to Louisa, as if her own daughter were a tourist listening to one of her famous talks on local geography and history.

Her mother didn't mention it, but the Cooper River Bridge in her story was not the wide concrete six-lane road of a bridge it is today—a chunk of Interstate 26 lofted over the river—with reversible lanes and concrete walls to block the view and keep you safe. Crossing the new bridge you might as well be flying over the river in an armchair. The old bridge, however, which stood beside the new one for a few years and carried traffic one way into the city from the north, was once the only bridge coming or going: a narrow two-lane steel girder bridge with rusty open railings (like some rickety roller coaster at a county fair) through which you could look down onto the wings of gulls and the rusty barges, sailboats, tankers and, now and then, the periscope of a submarine heading down river from the navy base toward the harbor and the open ocean.

That was the bridge Mamie had to cross with their family every summer on the way to the beach house and her room underneath the house where she slept on a rusty iron bed and fixed her hair in front of a mirror with most of the silver peeled off. All day she picked crab meat from the bushels of crabs the family hauled in. She peeled shrimp, cooked, walked the children to the beach, swept the sand out of the house. At night, she read her Bible loudly to herself or sang and ironed in front of the oscillating fan.

"Well, old Mamie had an absolute and utter terror of that bridge," Mother said. She was launched now, Louisa saw, there would be no turning back. Louisa pushed her needle harder through the stiff linen. "Something about being high up in the air like that, crossing water, scared her so much that when I told her it was time to get ready to go to the beach, those little bitty pigtails she used to wear would practically stand straight out from her head, and she'd fall to her knees and start wringing her hands. 'Lord, Missis,' she'd wail. 'Lord God. Leave me back behind on solid earth. I too old. Be crossing that water soon enough.' I'd tell her I'd carry her request to my husband, but I knew it wouldn't do any good. He never would put up with nonsense from the help. 'She'll ride with us, as usual,' he always said. 'I'm not going to inconvenience my family to accommodate Mamie's superstitions.'

Was this a story of historic and ongoing injustice, Louisa asked herself? Not likely. In the 1960s when the concept of injustice finally intruded on their world, her mother had been outraged. "Injustice?" Mother would say. "What injustice? We carried them all those years. We looked out for them." She came from that generation whose childhoods had touched the rim of the time in which their opinions about race still felt like facts. Such as: The Hilliards had been good masters, kind masters who seldom raised the whip to their people, which was why, after they were freed, Teneh and Cuff, Binah, Scipio, Daniel and Abby and Maum Harriette, Mamie's mother, had stayed on at Fairview. The Hilliards take care of their own, this story went. When Mamie's husband King got drunk and cut a man at a juke joint on Calhoun Street, hadn't Hugh Marion, Sr. bailed him out of jail?

"Let me ask you this," her mother would say. "After Mamie's daughter died, who allowed Evelyn to come live with her grandmother?" They didn't have to do that Mother insisted, or let Mamie stay in the kitchen house in their yard either, for that matter. Even after Evelyn ran off that way and left them in the lurch, who drove Mamie up to that girl's graduation from South Carolina State? Louisa herself, that's who. Round and round the stories went, round and round like miraculous wheels that never warped or splintered as they rolled through time.

When the civil rights movement came to Charleston, the striking hospital workers lined King Street, singing and chanting, holding their signs: FREE-DOM NOW. WE SHALL NOT BE MOVED. Evelyn had marched into Pierce Bros. department store, which did not serve Negroes, and asked to try on a pair of shoes. Louisa's mother had been personally hurt and affronted that blacks should resent the cordial and correct distance the races had agreed to keep from one another, the obvious and necessary ranking that kept them in the separate worlds they had always lived in so comfortably.

One night during that unsettled time, Hugh fell into a bitter mood after his fifth trip to the cut-glass decanter of port on the dining room sideboard. "Keep Mother away from the windows, Sister," he said. "She's liable to ask Martin Luther King if he's looking for yard work." She might have, too. Mother was as invulnerable to the idea of injustice as a turtle tucked into its shell.

So her mother's story was definitely not about injustice. "Well, for about two weeks before we left for the beach there were some odd comings and goings around our kitchen house," she said. "Mamie's pastor must have visited her half a dozen times. Then there were the other characters. That old scarecrow of a man who used to run errands for us. The vegetable cart man. A one-eyed woman who sold baskets down at the market. You'd hear them knocking on the screen door of the kitchen house all hours of the day or night. 'Aunt Mamie,' they'd call. 'Aunt Mamie.' But we knew what they were—root doctors and so forth—bringing charms to her." She leaned forward, confiding in her daughter. "We pretended we didn't know," she said. "But we did. On the morning of our departure, Mamie would appear with her Bible clutched in one hand, her suitcase in the other. She'd have her lucky dime on a string around her ankle, nutmeg around her neck along with a big silver cross on a red ribbon and a cloth pouch she'd sewed. She would never tell us what was in it. Graveyard dirt, I suppose. They were big on that. Crab claws, maybe. I always had to turn my back to keep from laughing at the poor old thing and hurting her feelings.

"Mamie sat in the back between you and Hugh. As soon as we started up the bridge, she'd grab the door handle with one hand and the rope across the back of the front seat with the other. Remember that big, black, sixteen-cylinder Buick we owned, your father's pride and joy? Remember the little ropes across the backs of the seats? Up we'd go onto the bridge, with Mamie hanging on for dear life, with her eyes squeezed shut, praying. 'Sweet Jesus! Lord have mercy! Great God! Do, Jesus! Great King!' I think she used up every name they have for their God before we'd gotten over the first span. She'd start off muttering to herself—she knew your father didn't want to listen to her foolishness—but before we'd reached the top of the first span, she'd practically be shouting.

Of course I'd see what was coming by the way your father scowled into the rearview mirror, and then all of a sudden, he'd speak. 'Mamie,' he'd say, so quietly *I* almost couldn't hear him, and I was sitting right next to him in the front seat, but Mamie would jump like he'd grabbed her. 'Do I need to remind you that you are riding in my family car?'

"'No suh,' she'd say, 'sure don't,' and all the while she'd be studying the floor with her bottom lip poking out about a mile. Mamie was light skinned—*high yellow* we called them—with refined features and hazel eyes and a few freckles across her nose and cheeks. But she sure prayed like an African. Well, after your father reprimanded her, she'd simmer down and mumble her prayers to herself until we were safely across the bridge and down onto Mt. Pleasant. Old Mamie. Didn't she make the best biscuits?"

And right there, her mother stopped, as though the thread had run off the spool. She nodded emphatically, smoothed the skirt of her bathrobe down over her knees and stared out at the bridges until her eyelids began to droop. This drowsiness was Louisa's signal that the visit was over. Mother would not talk again that day. She had come to the end of the story; there was nothing more to tell. It was time for Louisa to fold up the linen banner and pack it away in her portmanteau along with her embroidery floss and the pair of small silver scissors, its handles shaped like the outstretched necks and heads of cranes in flight, that had belonged to her ancestor Eliza Hilliard, another spinster seamstress. Time to help her mother out of the wheelchair and into the bed. Time to draw the covers up around her mother's neck, kiss the pink scalp that showed through the white mist of hair and tiptoe out of the room, closing the door behind her. Time to walk out into the morning air, the smell of fish and oil and sun on water, and to remember how the water had looked from the top of the highest span of the old Cooper River Bridge: like a floor, hard and glittering, swept with light.

It wasn't her mother's drifting canoe of a mind that had landed her in the nursing home; it was her body. One night earlier that spring Louisa had waked to her mother's call. Though her voice had thinned, it was sharp as a needle, and like a needle it pierced Louisa's sleep. "Louisa, Louisa, I need to tee-tee."

Sleep-clogged, stiff, Louisa dragged herself out of her canopied bed in the upstairs corner room. Snapping on the light in the bedroom next to hers, she found her mother propped on pillows on the chintz-covered chaise lounge where she slept upright to ease her breathing. Oxygen tubes ran up her nose, a wheeled canister of oxygen sat on the floor beside the chair.

Louisa meant no disrespect when she thought of her mother as grotesque. One hundred and two, her face like a pudding, she was bloated from medications and edema and from an appetite which she hadn't even attempted to control since her husband died. No sooner had Hugh Marion, Sr. gone to rest in St. Phillips churchyard than she began to pour half-and-half on her breakfast cereal, stir four thick pats of butter into every plate of rice, order her shrimp cooked in melted butter and bacon grease. Now she was hung with slabs, folds, and pouches of fat, as if she were outfitting herself in flesh for a long trip into a land of famine.

As Mother ballooned, so did her stubbornness, the imperial selfishness (this much resentment, and no more, Louisa would allow herself) that made her deaf to her doctor's warnings. "My God, Elizabeth," he'd say. "You've gained another fifteen pounds. This must stop." She wouldn't accept a wheelchair, either, or allow Louisa to hire someone to help them. Absolutely not. If the tip of Mother's cane marred the floors, the floors would be refinished. If in the middle of the night her mother decided to work a crossword puzzle and needed a four-letter synonym for *decaying plant matter* or a reminder of the precise location of the cruet stand, Louisa would pull on her bathrobe and help her find them.

As for hiring help, her mother's refusal rested on historical precedent. Elizabeth's mother Juliana had cared for *her* mother; now Louisa would care for hers, and in this way, a shining vein of loyalty and devotion would run through dark and crumbling time. Sometime that spring, watching her mother's jaws roll as she munched toast, watching her lips reach for the rim of the coffee cup and suck the hot liquid in, Louisa decided that to call her grotesque (privately, of course, and only to herself) was simply to state a fact, something with which Louisa had made the firmest and longest-lasting relationship of her life.

On the night of the bathroom call, Louisa knelt and forced her mother's feet into a pair of mustard-colored corduroy loafers from Woolworth's, the kind that Mother had never allowed Mamie to wear around the house because they slapped against her heels with such a slovenly sound. Size twelve and still the heel had to be cut away to keep them from hurting her mother's swollen feet. Hoisting her mother up off the bed, Louisa said "Upsy-daisy," just to hear the playful lilt of those words. She rolled the oxygen tank with one hand, kept the other arm around her mother's waist as they struggled and staggered toward the bathroom at the far end of the hall. Louisa felt her mother's weight sag against her, felt her damp armpits and clammy neck, the warm rush of her breath. It was too hot for this work, but Mother always ordered the air conditioning shut off at 8 P.M. sharp and the windows opened—even when it was still stifling outside and the air so muggy it seeped through the screens like fog through a sieve.

"We're going to fall. We're going to collapse right here in the middle of the hall," Louisa thought as they inched toward the bathroom and she felt the beginning of a panicky tightening in her lungs.

But they didn't collapse in the hall. They made it to the bathroom and then, as she tried to ease her mother down onto the toilet, holding her around the waist with one arm while her mother grappled with her underpants, Louisa slipped. To keep herself from falling she let go of her mother, who sat down hard on the floor and whimpered like a baby. When Louisa couldn't get her mother up, and the old woman could no longer hold back her water, Louisa put down two towels. She turned her back while Mrs. Elizabeth Hilliard Marion peed on the bathroom floor in the house where Hilliards had journeyed from birth to death for more than two centuries.

When her mother was done, Louisa picked up the wet towels and dropped them down the laundry chute in the bathroom closet. Then she called 911 from the phone in the upstairs hall. "My mother has fallen in the bathroom," she said, "and I can't get her up."

After she came back from making the call, Louisa sat on the cool tile floor and leaned against the toilet, holding her mother, who dozed with her head lolling against Louisa's shoulder and one hand splayed out on her cheek as if she were dismayed or ashamed. The thin hiss of the oxygen tubes in her mother's nose was the only sound in the room besides the whine of a mosquito that had found them. Her mother dozed, her chin pillowed in the fat of her neck, and as the siren came toward them through the night, Louisa looked down and saw the slack, puckered elastic of her mother's yellowed nylon underpants. She heard a click, like a gear engaging, and then an ominous dizzying sense of acceleration as though time itself had sped up.

Before this night, age had only nibbled at Louisa. In cold, rainy weather, her knuckles swelled and ached. Her hips felt stiff every morning. Some days the musty smell of her pillow startled her. Or the smell that rose from her mouth when she flossed her teeth, that carried her back to her grandmother and what had been on her breath. How foreign those smells had seemed then, how familiar now. There were the migrating patches of numbness and constriction, the fine lines around her mouth into which her lipstick spread. Signs of aging, true, but never too many to manage with dignity.

Propped up against the toilet on the bathroom floor with her mother, she'd felt old all over, as though she were curing in age, like the nineteenth-century Hilliard Madeira and peach brandy still curing in barrels down in the cellar. Both of them, herself and the liquor, steeped in time, which caused the collapse of one and deepened the flavor and value of the other. And she wept for the two old women they'd become. Two old women with their stains and flows. Two old women and the younger unable to help the older get up from the floor or pull her nightgown down to cover her underpants and slack thighs and ugly slippers.

The ambulance attendants would no doubt notice all of those things, and later, in some Waffle House up on Ashley Phosphate Road, they'd shake their heads and laugh about the old ladies they'd hauled up off the bathroom floor of their house in the historic district. "They pee just like the rest of us," one of them would say and the whole place would crack up. That night, after the vision of the Waffle House faded, Louisa laid her cheek down on her mother's head and whispered, "Mother, don't you think it's time to move on?"

Later she wondered if her mother heard her, because the week after the bathroom crisis, at their doctor's insistence, she went quietly to the nursing home. She even sent Louisa a note, in shaky handwriting that trickled down her heavy cream notepaper, thanking her daughter for finding her such a nice house to live in. Quiet and clean, it did not smell, and the help were the courteous, almost invisible, old-fashioned colored people you seldom found working anywhere anymore. The woman who ran the home was a woman like herself, Louisa thought, a *discreet matron* as they used to call themselves in the newspaper advertisements offering music or sewing or watercolor lessons for young ladies.

Her mother had been in the home for three months when the owner called in the middle of the night. "Miss Marion," she said, "I'm sorry, but I must inform you that your mother has passed away." Even while the woman went on talking (just died, she said, about half an hour ago) Louisa felt restless. Her brother needed to be told about their mother, and as his older sister, she was the one to make the call. Besides, she needed to talk to someone. The news of her mother's death had gone into her and started growing, pushing everything else out until it was just a big, spinning hollow place inside, like the swirling cloud of wind on a hurricane tracking map, and she was in danger of dropping into this place alone. "I'll be right there," she said, "but first I must call my brother."

She switched on the gooseneck lamp on the telephone table in the hall and took her address book out of the drawer. She turned the pages quickly, looking for Hugh's page, while fear rose insider her, hissing softly like Mother's oxygen. She had to find his number before she got lost in the fear. At last, there it was. HUGH, she'd printed in block letters across the top. His addresses, entered and crossed out, filled the entire page. The apartment on King Street where he'd moved after he dropped out of law school at the University of South Carolina. The house on the marsh on Isle of Palms where he lived one summer, renting floats from a little shack on the beach made of pine boards covered with palmetto fronds. The apartment near the Navy base in North Charleston, where it was never quite clear what he did. The house on Station Creek in McClellanville.

Hugh had laughed when he told her about the twitching carpet of termites on every floor of the house the real estate agent showed him, how he'd waded through them and rented the house anyway. It was so close to the creek that the full-moon spring and autumn tides swirled up under the house. Hugh had pulled his bateau up onto the mud bank there and tied it to one of the brick pillars that supported the front porch. He spent his days fishing, crabbing, drinking, drifting down the tidal creeks in his bateau. Sometimes he boiled big kettles of shrimp—loaves and fishes, he called them—to feed the multitudes who came to parties that went on for days. That's how much they loved him. One time he called at two in the morning to invite her, a chaos of merriment roaring behind his voice, and when she refused, he turned maudlin. She was his sister, he said, his only sister. Why wouldn't she come and party with him?

This had been in the late sixties, early seventies, and what Hugh had really been doing was unloading marijuana off the boats that slipped up the creeks near McClellanville, then running the dope down to Charleston to sell. Hugh was getting rich at it, too, refilling the bank account he'd drained so quickly of the money their father had left him. When the state drug agents set out to break up the smuggling along that part of the coast, they went to the Charleston real estate agencies that sold houses in the historic district and collected the names of people who'd made cash down payments. They did the same at marinas and luxury car dealerships. The Mercedes-Benz dealership in North Charleston gave them Hugh's name, but they never did catch up with him. He moved too fast.

Then with a shudder she was fully awake, and Hugh was twenty years dead. She closed the address book and put it back in the drawer, turned off the lamp. With one hand on the wall, she found her way back to her room, where she sat on the edge of her bed and rocked a little, getting ready. The hall's darkness seemed to flow into the room. It smelled of old wood and wet air, something green drifting through it. The smell of ghosts, Mamie always said. She wouldn't go into the upstairs hall at night, with all those ghosts jostling and crowding one another. "Black and white, all jam up together," was how Mamie described the scene. One time, Mamie said, a witch jumped on her back in the hall and rode her down the stairs and out into the yard, where she shook it off and stuffed it down the well.

Louisa remembered the feel of Mamie's fingers plucking at her sleeve. "Walk over this side the hall, Miss," she'd say, and Louisa would know they were detouring around one of her ancestors, or Mamie's. She'd find Mamie standing on the brick front walk, broom in hand, staring up at the chimney. "They pouring out now, Miss," Mamie would say. "Just like smoke."

As soon as the owner opened the front door, Louisa was grateful to her. Here it was the middle of the night, and the woman was dressed in a navy blue shirtwaist dress and low-heeled pumps. Her hair was combed, her lipstick was on straight. She carried papers in her hand as though she'd been at work for hours. No bathrobe, no straggling hair or slack, bewildered face to show that death had surprised her. "Thank you for your discretion," was all Louisa could think to say.

"I'm going to let you talk to Yvonne, the nurse's aide who was on duty when your mother passed away," the woman said as she and Louisa climbed the stairs and started down the hall toward her mother's room. The moon cast the shape of the window at the other end of the hall ahead of them as they walked, and Louisa listened for her mother's voice calling Mamie, but it was quiet except for the shushing of their feet on the carpet.

In her mother's room, the bedside lamp was turned low. A woman sat in a rocking chair beside the bed, rocking and stroking the spread over her mother's shoulder and humming to herself. When Louisa came in, she stood up, smoothing down her uniform. Louisa saw a gold front tooth, a quick, kind smile.

"This is Mrs. Marion's daughter, Yvonne," the owner said and backed out of the room, closing the door behind her with a soft click.

"She was a sweet, fine lady," Yvonne said. "See here how peaceful she look." She touched the dead woman's cheek. "You blessed," she said. "Some struggle and fight." Yvonne had checked on her mother at midnight, then gone down the hall to look in on someone else, and when she'd come back at 12:45, her mother had *ceased to breathe,* Yvonne said, as if, Louisa thought, those strangely formal words could manage the fact.

"So she didn't say anything?"

"Not as I am aware of."

"Thank you for all you've done," Louisa said, anxious for the woman to leave, and when Yvonne had gone, she sat down on the bed. Her mother lay on her back with her eyes closed, the sheet neatly folded over the blanket and pulled up her under her chin. They'd disconnected the oxygen tubes from her nose and rolled the canister into the corner of the room. On her mother's upper lip, Louisa saw the outline of the tape that had held the oxygen line in place. She licked her thumb to scrub it off, then stopped. The undertaker would clean that mark away, she thought. He would clean away all the marks of life. That was his job. Hers, it seemed, was to abide on this bed while the wake of her mother's passing rocked her like a boat.

Her mother's face looked as satisfied as it did every time she found Mamie's biscuits at the end of the story about the bridge. It occurred to Louisa that at the moment of death her mother might even have been dreaming of Mamie's biscuits. She remembered that they felt dense and warm in your hand, then dissolved like buttery clouds when you bit into them. So maybe it was comfort her mother had been looking for in that endlessly repeated story—comfort and certainty in the memory of those biscuits and of Mamie's silly old colored-woman terrors, so much more primitive and obscure than their own.

Sitting beside her mother's body, Louisa felt she'd entered another world of silence and stillness that lapped out from the body on the bed and surrounded her. It was the stillness, the vacancy that she could not bend her mind around. She almost said, "Mother?" the way she used to do, to wake her. But she brushed back wisps of hair from her mother's forehead and kept still. She picked up her mother's cool hand and held it between both of her own.

Whatever life is, she saw, it visits the body, then goes, taking nothing you could catch, store in a bottle, or press and keep under glass. Taking nothing you could see and taking everything. She remembered a darkened room stuffed with summer heat, the wooden shutters latched over the windows and herself sick with diphtheria on the canopied bed, the cool feel of her mother's fingers rubbing hand cream on her lips. The last person who could say, "When you were a baby . . . " and show her a glimpse of herself as she'd been before she knew what it meant to exist.

Looking up, Louisa saw the lights of the Cooper River bridges and thought about Hugh, crossing the new bridge on his way to the beach house on Sullivan's Island. He'd forced a door, rummaged in drawers, drank half a bottle of port, sat in every chair and lay on every bed. For weeks the restless twist of his body stayed in the white chenille bedspreads. Then he'd driven his silver Mercedes up onto the dunes in front of the house until the tires sank in the sand and shot himself in the head.

Looking at the bridges, remembering Hugh, she felt afraid again. To this day, whenever she crossed that bridge, her throat tightened, her heart beat slow and hard. A bright, merciless light seemed to shine into her eyes, and she wanted only to make it safely to the other side. She remembered her mother's story: all of them in the car together, traveling safely across the water. She remembered

Mamie's prayers and her father's outburst. She was the only survivor of those who'd lived that story. It was her story now, and there was no comfort in it, for she also remembered how her father had grown philosophical after he'd silenced Mamie. Looking down at the water, he'd said the same thing every time.

Water would feel like concrete if you fell into it from this height, he'd say. And just like that, how high they were turned into how far they could fall, and silent as one of Mamie's ghosts, the knowledge of their actual and precarious place on earth accompanied them to the other side.

Keep Talking

I saved a man's life. That's a fine place to begin, and what makes the story even better, I didn't really know him. He was a neighbor, that's all, the man who lived across the street in the gray house under the hickory tree. Every Monday night, if we happened to be rolling our garbage cans to the curb at the same time, we spoke. Sometimes twin girls raked the front yard or ran in circles or jumped rope. In cool weather, they wore matching pink jackets and white plastic bows clipped to the ends of their short, stiff pigtails. Most days, the curtains stayed drawn across the front picture window, as though someone worked a night shift and slept all day. Every Wednesday afternoon, a woman carried a laundry basket into the side yard and clipped a row of brown pants and shirts to the clothesline.

The day I saved his life, I'd taken my son blackberry picking at a friend's farm, or what my friend and her husband *called* their farm, in hopes, I think, that it might someday live up to the name. On the day we went blackberry picking, the farm was just a piece of land healing from hard use. The last owners had cut down all the big oaks, hickories and pines and sold them for timber. Now the sweet gum, scrub oak and spindly pine grew in thin groves all over the land, and cat brier and stinging nettle covered the hard, dry ground beneath the trees. And yet, somehow, down in the eroded gullies and up along the cracked ridges, there were thickets of blackberries. That June the branches were laden with fruit.

Oblivious to thorns and scratches, my three-year-old son ran from bush to bush, squatting and peering into each thorny tangle as though the bush were a door into some enchanted place. Time after time, he reached in through the thorns and found the fattest, the blackest, the sweetest fruit. All afternoon he came back without a scratch, opened his hands and spilled fat berries into our bucket, his eyes lustrous with happiness.

At home, I carried him into the house asleep. My husband put him in his bed, and just as I was bending down to kiss his blackberry stained chin, I heard a scream, and from our front window I saw my neighbor's wife standing under the hickory tree. "Help me, please help me," she screamed. Then a tumble, a flood of garbled words. And my first thought as I ran down the front steps was nothing to be proud of. I was *angry* at the woman, I wanted to shake her. "Stop screaming," I wanted to shout. "No one can understand you when you're screaming."

The second thought was worse. As I ran, a TV news story began to roll inside my head. You know the one I mean. Yellow crime-scene tape, flashing lights, a body on a gurney, the neighbors crowding around for a turn at the microphone. *In Southeast Atlanta tonight,* this story begins, *a woman was lured to a neighbor's house by cries for help, then robbed and shot to death.* Why? No one could say. The first person in line steps up. *Good neighbors,* she says. *Good Christian people. Kids, jobs, everything.* When everyone has had their say, the neighbors leave the scene and go home to tell the story to anyone who missed it. Tomorrow, the kids will carry the story to school, and the grown-ups will take it to the cafeteria serving-line or the desk in a tall, downtown building or out to the mall and tell it to anyone who'll listen. They'll spread this virus of a story to other people who will carry it home to their families who will carry it out to other homes and families, until we've got a pandemic on our hands and half the world is infected by this emergency we're living, this guerrilla war we're fighting, where everyone is the enemy so you can't trust anyone, you just can't risk it.

At the foot of their steps she grabbed my arm. "My husband—here—home from the hospital on a pass—Oh, God." Her hands flapped toward the screen door. I eased it open, stepped onto the porch. He was sprawled on the porch floor as though someone had dropped him there. Black shoes, thin socks, black pants, a hospital wristband, a white knit shirt, a narrow face and eyes that stared into empty distance. She'd slipped a pillow under his head. The shadows of leaves moved over his face. I put my hand on his chest and felt something stir. "Call 911," I said, and then I went to work.

Airways, breathing, circulation. ABC. I'd learned that formula in a Red Cross class I took when my son was a baby and I became frantic with fear that I might find him unconscious in his crib and lose him because I hadn't mastered the simple alphabet of life. The instructor promised that if we memorized the steps this way they would come back to us in a crisis, and she was right. She was *right.* I almost laughed when I remembered them. ABC. The siren was getting close as I tipped back the man's head and breathed into his mouth. Five breaths, ten, then five chest compressions, and as the ambulance stopped in the front of the house, the man's chest began to rise and fall. The EMTs ran down the driveway. A minute later they had him on a gurney, loaded into the ambulance and gone.

The man came home from the hospital in late June, and every afternoon for a few weeks afterwards, he sat in a lawn chair in the side yard with his eyes closed, his face turned toward the sun. Then one day he got up from his chair, bent down and picked up a stick and then he paused, as if to see what his heart thought of that. By August he was mowing the grass, and when fall came, he raked the leaves under his hickory tree and hauled them in bags to the curb. Before Thanksgiving he planted bulbs, and the next spring a drift of King Alfred daffodils, gold as lacquered sunlight, came up under that tree.

Late one gray, cold December afternoon, as I walked up the driveway toward my house, and he walked from his car toward his, a flock of grackles descended on the hickory tree and rioted there for a minute or two, filling the air with the noise of a thousand, rusty, turning gears. Then, as suddenly as they'd landed they all flew away, the sun came out and turned our street into a river of light, winding, slowly, somewhere. When he looked over at me again, he was smiling. We waved, we hesitated, as if one of us were about to walk over and begin the conversation that only we could have about what had happened to us both on the day he didn't die. *Tell me,* I might have said. *When your life is given back to you, do you call it a gift?*

I wish this was true. I wish my neighbor was alive and I was a hero, but he's not and I'm not and the truth is: my neighbor died on his porch that day. No one could have saved him, one of the EMTs said when I asked. I had to know because I hadn't tried.

He didn't sit with his face turned to the summer sun; no King Alfred daffodils came up in his yard. The grackles descended and flew away, a river of light poured down our street, but he wasn't there to see it. I asked around the neighborhood: What was wrong with him? He'd been to church that morning, a neighbor said. They had the best service. They clapped and sang and praised the Lord, and he came home happy, sat down on the porch and then he died. Something in his chest, they said. Lungs or heart.

Now the part about my son is true. The trip to the country. The miracle of the blackberries. The man's wife and how she screamed—*Oh, God, here, my husband, please*—the TV news story in my head, that all happened. But the man was dead when I got there. There was blood in his mouth and he was so empty and still. I knelt beside him and touched his neck, his wrist, put my hand on his chest and felt a stirring that I told myself was his heart. I saw a falling-away in his eyes, felt his body slacken and subside. His wife wore a white dress and tennis shoes; she held a blue comb in her hand and tapped it against her palm as she looked up and down the street. "You think I should put him in the car and take him back to St. Joseph's?" she said. "They let him out on a pass. I'm supposed to have him back by seven o'clock. What time is it now?"

"It's three," I said. I kept my hand on his chest, and then I remembered what I'd heard a doctor say about how to help the grievously wounded, the dying, the dead. "Talk to them," he said. "If they're still alive, they can hear you. Hearing is the last sense to go."

So I told the man we had blackberries. I said he could have some to eat in a bowl with sugar and cream. *Blackberries, sugar, cream.* Maybe he wasn't dead when I said those words; maybe they carried him through one last moment of fear before the world went blank and the words stopped. While we waited for the ambulance, a storm moved through. Thunder rattled the windows of the house, then rain fell in fat drops that tore the leaves and struck the ground hard. When it was over, and the sun came out again and gilded the wet pavement. The shadows of leaves flowed across his face. He looked on in blank astonishment at the green, wet world.

I used to believe that death came from somewhere beyond this world. In order for it to come in, there had to be a kicked-in door, a broken window, some violence or omen. I believed that if death walked into the room you would know it right away. It would look like a thief or the grim reaper, one of those masks we pin over death's blank human face.

I learned my neighbor's name when a policeman printed it on the top line of a form. "James Earl Turner," his wife said, hands over her face, my arm around her shoulders. A crowd of neighbors had gathered and stood watching.

The officer lifted the edge of the sheet covering the body and filled in another line. I could not save my neighbor, not with my hands and not with my breath or my Red Cross ABCs. Even in this story, the man dies. But I have caught him on his outbound flight and given him a few possibilities to pass through on his way to the end of all possibility. The man is dead and gone, and death is everywhere and anytime.

What do you do with those cold facts? You keep talking, that's all. Spin words around your neighbor whom no love or hope can save, a net to hold him as he falls.

Birth Mother

It's been a month since the judge in Parkersburg made them a family, and now they're driving from West Virginia to Port Huron, Michigan, to celebrate the adoption with some friends of their new parents. In the van heading north, Cody curls under a blanket on the seat that folds down into a bed, his pillow from home bunched under his head. Cory's *trip coma* his new mother and father call it, the way he goes to sleep at the start of a long ride and wakes up to stumble in and out of service station bathrooms, in and out of restaurants, until they get where they're going and he wakes up for good. In the next seat, his sister Beth nods to music that trickles from the headphones clamped over her ears. Her fingers comb the mane and tail of a plastic, dappled-gray Appaloosa, its bridle and saddle long gone, that she must take with her wherever she goes. She's seven, big-eyed and skinny, with long brown hair that used to be tangled and dirty but now hangs brushed and clean to her shoulders.

From one of the tall front seats, their mother turns around to look at him and Beth, leans over to talk to their father, and then they both laugh. Mother. Father. He's getting used to calling them that, but he corrects himself right after—*new parents*. Their new mother has a delicate beautiful face, short blonde hair, shining eyes. Beth says she looks like a fairy princess. Their father is a giant with a big, black beard and a loud laugh. Mother. Father. The princess and the giant. Whoever they are, he's fooled them into thinking he's sleeping. Dreaming, yes, but not sleeping. He lets the van's stuffy, coffee-smelling warmth and the rhythmic thump of the tires over the spacers on the highway pull him down into the twilight behind his eyes where his real mother moves and he follows her.

At ten, he's the oldest. They've been out of their mother's house since Beth was three and he was six, living in foster homes along the Ohio River in Kanawha and Pettyville, while they waited for their mother to do something called *getting her life together* and come back for them. Now they have a new family, a permanent family; that's a promise, these grown-ups say. *Permanent. Promise.* He hears the words but their meaning flies away in a confusion of wings. Letters and words are a mystery to him, clocks and calendars, too. His teachers call to say he can't pay attention, he can't sit still. After those calls, he lies on the floor of his bedroom, listening through the heat vent while his new mother cries at the kitchen table downstairs and his new father talks to her in his deep, low voice. He feels their feeling for him, but in the middle of everything there's a stutter, a stumble, an emptiness he falls into, where he waits, quiet and small and hardly breathing.

It doesn't take much to start him thinking about his mother. Today, it's the way the sound of the tires changes from hum to whine. He pushes up on one elbow and sees that they're crossing a wide brown river. It looks like the river he and his mother crossed when he went to stay at her mother's house in Pomeroy, Ohio, while his mother went to the hospital and had Beth. Now he's riding with her again, the two of them rattling over the bridge in her rusty black pickup truck with the wind blowing through the open windows. He sees her pale green eyes and ragged blonde hair, the way she gnaws her bottom lip. They pull down his grandmother's rutted drive. The old lady is out in the garden beside the house, a tall woman with wide cheekbones and a cloud of white hair. Alma Richardson was her name. She wears a shapeless dress with belt-loops but no belt, and she stands between two rows of climbing beans, holding a bucket and squinting at the truck. His mother walks over to her and rests her head on Alma's chest. "Mama," she says.

The old lady pats her back. "You look about ready to pop," she says. "Whereabouts is that good for nothing man?"

He remembers his grandmother's backyard that sloped down to the river, the way the leaves of the buckeye trees hung dusty and still. On the back porch outside the kitchen door, under a sagging string that held some rags and a gigantic pair of white underpants, lay a dead snapping turtle with dried green algae on its armored shell. He nudged the carcass with his foot and his grandmother came up behind him and gripped his shoulders with her strong, boney hands. On the river, a barge horn groaned. "When your mama gets gone, we're going to have us some good old snapper soup," she whispered in his ear.

Later, he ran through the house, carrying a green medicine bottle he'd found under the back porch. He tripped over the doorjamb, the bottle hopped out of his hand and smashed on the floor in front of his grandmother's rocking chair in the living room. The chair stopped rocking. The TV laughed. "Boy, I swear," his grandmother said. From the floor beside her chair, she picked up a tin can with the label peeled off. She brought the can up close to her face and a thin brown stream ran out of her mouth and into the can. Her pale blue eyes never left his face. His mother heaved herself up from the mustard colored sofa and came toward him, one hand under her belly, the other cocked to slap, but his grandmother's voice cracked out. "Leave him be, why don't you?" His mother went away soon after, but she came back that time.

"Your birth mother's name was Norma Lee Richardson," his new mother said the night before they left on this trip, while he and Beth looked through the pictures and papers she kept in a special wooden box with two hearts carved into the lid. Hearing her name, he felt the stumble again, the fall into watchful stillness. *Birth mother* was what he and Beth were supposed to call their mother now, as though there were temporary mothers and permanent mothers and a judge could change one into another.

"Where is my mother now?" he asked that night. *Mother,* not birth mother, to let his new mother know where she stood with him.

"Somewhere on the river, Cody," she said. "The last anybody heard, she was living in a shelter over in Gallipolis."

Shelter. The word brought a picture to his mind: he and his mother and Alma out in her garden picking tomatoes when a black cloud came hulking up over the river. "Best take shelter," his grandmother said, and she grabbed his hand and led him toward the house through the first, fat raindrops while his mother lumbered along behind. No sooner were they all inside than the rain broke like a wave against the house. While the trees thrashed and the rain thundered on the roof, the three of them sat at Alma's kitchen table with the radio on and he drank a Coke and watched the two of them play a card game.

Beth calls their new mother "Mom" all the time now, as though she's accepted that their real mother was the temporary kind. But she's wrong, and she gets other things wrong, too. She swears their mother was fat. Beth's mother had missing teeth and skaggy hair that was sometimes red and sometimes white-blonde with black roots. Beth's mother had a mean laugh and a hard hand. But what did Beth know? Before their mother got fat with Beth, she was so thin she wore his pants when hers needed washing. He remembers her ribs and hipbones and the sharp collarbone that hurt when she hugged him tight. He remembers the single pink foam curler she wore in the front of her hair on the days she got up in time to drive him to the babysitter's on the way to her job at the Huddle House.

He remembers how good she smelled then. The little gold cross around her neck. Her pink lipstick and silvery green eyeshadow. Other mornings she was running late, so she left him in the white house near Raven Rock. She locked the doors and told him to stay inside, not to touch the stove or answer the phone unless it rang three times, stopped, and rang again. He remembers walking from room to room while the phone rang and milky light leaked in through the plastic she'd taped over the windows when it got cold.

Beth was just a baby when their grandmother Alma died and her rocking chair came across the river in the back of an uncle's pickup one summer morning, along with the mustard colored couch and some boxes of dishes and clothes and pictures of Jesus. How many times after that had he tiptoed downstairs in the pitch-black dark and found his mother rocking in Alma's chair, rocking and crying and drinking beer?

"Mama," he heard her say quietly one time. "Oh, Mama."

He remembers standing in the doorway and watching her cigarette glow and fade until she saw him and set down her beer and held out her hand to him.

"What are you doing awake, little man?" she said. Her voice sounded so very tender then. If the night itself could speak, it would have sounded like his mother on those nights when she rocked in Alma's chair and he stood close to her for a minute until she nudged him away. "Go on back to bed now, baby," she said. "You don't need to worry about this grown-up mess."

Right here is where he needs to slow the story down because this is where it speeds up and threatens to run away from him. He can tell they're coming into a city now. Outside, it's getting dark and the lights beside the highway are coming on and making a curved river of lights they're riding.

"Motor City, kids," their dad calls back. He's getting used to these people and their habits now. His new father wants to teach them everything about everything, so he'd better pay attention. Cody pushes up on one elbow and looks out the window. Beth takes off her headphones and puts them in her lap and folds her hands, looking interested, the way she does at school. It scares him that she's such a little kiss-ass. She'll run up to anyone who smiles at her and jump into their arms. He's tried to teach her to hold back, but she wants everybody to like her. And if they don't, sometimes she throws up.

Now he sees tall steel smokestacks and buildings with thousands of small, lighted windows. "They make cars here," his father says. "Our van could have been made right out there. The people in those buildings work on what's called *assembly lines*," he says. "The cars come by on a big slow moving belt and one person attaches a piece of chrome, then the next person tightens a bolt. There are people out there," he says, "who spend their entire lives tightening the same bolt over and over."

"Don't they get bored?" Cody asks, watching the lighted windows stream past.

"I imagine they do," his new father says, but he's never bored. He's always making plans to take them somewhere, show them something. His footsteps shake the floor as he paces around the kitchen and talks on the phone. He's the principal of the elementary school where Cody and Beth don't go because they both need a smaller classroom, more individual attention. He's heard that talked about through the floor vent, too. Their new father makes a difference in a lot of children's lives, their new mother says, and she tells it as though she likes that about him, the way he says the kids at the high school love his wife, the librarian.

Light flares behind some of the windows, as though big sparklers are going off inside. "I bet it's hot in there," Cody says.

"Oh, man, don't you know it," his father says. "Loud, too." Then he starts to sing. "Last night I went to sleep in Dee-troit City / And I dreamed about those cotton fields back home."

Cody lies down again and yanks the pillow over his head, but that doesn't stop Beth's father Jerry from swaggering into his mind, singing like he thought he was good at it. Thinking about Jerry is dangerous; it makes his heart pound, but to find his mother, he has to slip past Jerry, and Jerry won't budge, so it helps to imagine working on the assembly line in one of those buildings, tightening the same bolt a million times, bored out of his mind.

Not long after Alma died, Jerry started hanging around their house in Raven Rock and going out with Cody's mother at night while Cody stayed home with the doors locked. And then one day a muddy red pickup truck with a crumpled front fender drove down their steep rutted drive and stopped in the front yard. Jerry was at the wheel, cracking his gum and smiling. He had blond hair swept back from a high white forehead, the smallest hands. He sat in the truck and blew the horn until Cody's mother came out of the house wearing tight black jeans, new black boots and a sweater the color of peaches. She ran down the porch steps and across the muddy yard. When she got to the truck she threw her arms around Jerry's neck and they kissed and kissed.

Jerry's two duffle bags went into his mother's room that day. The mustard colored couch in the living room was shoved aside and Jerry's green corduroy recliner was set in front of Jerry's TV. On the front porch, Jerry dropped a rusty log chain and a saw with a muddy orange cord attached. Looking at the pile, Cody decided that this tangle of things must be the *grown-up mess* he wasn't supposed to worry about.

Jerry moved into their house in the fall and not long after he came, Beth started growing in his mother's belly. ("You're gonna have you a brother or a sister, baby," his mother said, holding his face between both her hands, her smoky breath in his face. "Aren't you glad?") All fall, Jerry drove coal trucks and log trucks down the West Virginia Turnpike, and came home on the weekends. But around Thanksgiving, when the first snow fell, he came back to Raven Rock to stay. Cody curled in a sleeping bag on a mattress in an upstairs bedroom while music shook the floor under his head and his mother and Jerry laughed or shouted at one another downstairs. When Beth was born, they put her on a mattress with Cody and went back to partying.

How long did Jerry live with them? Long enough for Beth to crawl and then walk, her plastic diaper always loaded and slipping off her skinny butt. Long enough for Beth to grow a few teeth, for Beth's smell to become part of him: milk and dirty hair and dirty diaper and another smell that was like the smell that hung around the cotton candy machine at the fair. Long enough for them to learn the rules. No touching Jerry's truck or Jerry's person. No eating like slobs in front of Jerry. No noise when Jerry was sleeping. No sitting in Jerry's recliner. That was the most important rule of all, but Cody broke it anyway when Jerry and his mother went out. He liked to work the lever that made the footrest jump and the other lever that made the back fall down and pop straight up again. Whenever he and Beth crawled into it, he never meant to stay; they were just going to watch one TV show, but they always fell asleep and woke up with Jerry and their mother standing over them.

"Didn't I tell you not to be sitting in my chair, Cody?" Jerry said the first night caught him and Beth in the chair. The second time, Jerry dragged him out by the hair. "I mean it, little man," he said. "I catch you there again, I'll whip your ass." His eyes were light brown, nearly gold; they didn't exactly look at you, just drifted across your face and moved on.

"Come on, baby, leave him be," his mother said to Jerry in a tiny voice he'd never heard. She was wearing the peach-colored sweater and tight black jeans again. She put both arms around Jerry's neck and slipped a hand inside his shirt. "Stay out of Jerry's chair, Cody," she said over her shoulder as the two of them staggered out of the room.

A breeze wakes him and he sees that he's alone. All the van's doors are open and his sister is gone, his new mother and father, too. It serves him right. Sleep, and they leave you; wake, and they're gone. He jams his feet down into the athletic shoes that he wears with the laces always tied so he can slip them on fast. He jumps out of the van and finds himself in a grove of white trees with trembling leaves and the bark peeling off in long strips. Overhead, the sky is like a big blue balloon blown up tight and ahead, through the trees, there's only water. They're parked behind a small, yellow house. Down a steep bank, sun wobbles on the water. He follows the sound of grown up voices around the corner of the house and up the wooden steps to a deck where his mother and father and their friends sit around a wicker table, wine glasses in their hands. In the middle of the table a green plate holds some white cheese and round, brown crackers.

"There he is," his father says. "You were sound asleep, and we didn't want to wake you. Come say hello to the Bradleys. Come have something to eat."

Cody waves. "Hi." From the plate, he grabs three crackers and most of the cheese.

The grown-ups all laugh, and a tall man with a shiny bald spot on the top of his head waves back. The man wears khaki shorts and a light blue shirt with the sleeves rolled back over tanned arms. He raises his wine glass toward Cody. "Hey, buddy. Welcome," he says. On his right hand, he wears a square gold ring with letters on it. He remembers them now. This man, his father's friend, works for a bank in Charleston, the capitol of West Virginia. Whenever they're together, the man and his father stay up late and talk talk talk. His mother and Mrs. Bradley, too. All the grown-ups ever do when they're together is talk, eat, drink, laugh.

His new mother is wearing long silver earrings and a gold cardboard crown set with big rubies and emeralds, like the crowns you get at Burger King. Her bare feet are up on a chair and a wineglass rests on her stomach. He's never seen her look so happy. She grabs his hand, pulls him in, close to her softness that he wants to rest against so badly, but he shouldn't so he pulls back. "Nice hat," he says, and she puts up a hand to straighten the crown.

"Having you kids has made me feel like a queen, " she says and kisses him on the cheek before he can get away.

A short woman dressed in a white shirt and jeans, her brown hair pulled back into a ponytail, comes over and hugs him tight, then holds him away at arms length. "Look at you," she says. "Look how big you've gotten. You're almost as tall as I am."

"OK," he says, and stuffs the food into his mouth.

She turns his face back to hers, puts both hands on his shoulders and looks into his eyes. "We're glad you're here." Her eyes are brown and warm, and she has freckles sprinkled across her nose and cheeks. He can tell she's waiting for him to speak, but he doesn't know what to say, so he shrugs, his mouth full of crackers. He's like a puppy, he's heard his new mother say, he'll eat till he's sick if you don't stop him.

"Where's Beth?" he says, moving out from under her hands. His new dad points toward the lake where his sister squats at the end of a wooden dock that runs a little way out into the endless water. She holds out her hand to two Canada geese, and the grown-ups laugh. Beth is so dumb, she thinks a goose will come to her, like a dog. Their new mother calls him a hero, for looking after Beth in the foster homes, and now he has to keep her from being laughed at, so he takes the rest of his crackers and runs down toward the dock.

His room is on the front of the house, above the deck, his bed is pushed up under two windows that open onto the lake. The water there makes small lapping sounds. At night, the loons call and the grown-ups talk on the deck beneath his window. The Bradleys have no children, like his new mother and father had no children before he and Beth came. It seems there is sadness in not having children. Late at night, the word *adoption* goes around, like something they're passing from hand to hand. He hears glasses clink, the tenderness with which his name and Beth's are spoken. Every night he tries to stay awake in case they talk about his mother, but every night he falls asleep.

He doesn't remember falling asleep, but he does, and one night the dream comes again. His mother walks toward him across a parking lot in the snow, and the feeling begins to build the way it always does when he sees her, and he's mad and scared, excited and confused by everything he wants to say to her and doesn't know how to. She walks right up to him with her green eyes, her ragged hair, the little gold cross on a chain around her neck. She holds out her arms, and he walks into them and lays his head down on her chest. He hears her breathe, he hears her heart beating, and he knows the way you know sometimes in a dream, when nobody speaks but you hear the words anyway, that she's sorry for leaving him.

After supper on their last night at the lake, the grown-ups build a fire on the small sand beach near the dock, and they all sit around it on blankets. He and Beth are sandwiched between their new father and mother; the Bradleys across the fire. While the fire catches in the tent of sticks he helped his new father build, the grown-ups finish their plastic cups of wine and fill them again. His father and Mr. Bradley smoke cigars and make a big show of blowing smoke up into the air. When they're done, they crush the cigars in the sand. *Big-shots,* his mother used to call the men who crushed out their cigars in the hash browns she'd brought them, left a quarter on the table.

Mr. Bradley runs up the steps from the beach, two at a time, and a few minutes later, he's back, carrying a tray of graham crackers, a bag of marshmallows, a stack of Hershey's chocolate bars. Cody's mouth begins to water. Overhead, stars crowd the sky. He's never seen so many. The darker it gets, the more stars appear, and then a shining mist stretches like a scarf across the sky. The Milky Way, his father says. Imagine that you're standing on the edge, looking across. That's where we are in the Milky Way.

"Where?" he says.

"Right here."

He's turning two marshmallows on a stick in the fire, watching them bubble and brown, when he feels Beth getting evil beside him. She squirms, then inches her marshmallow closer and closer to his until finally, they touch and ooze together. That's when he turns on her. "Stop it, Beth," he says.

In the firelight, he sees Jerry's meanness on her face. "I'm going to te-elll," she sings. Everybody looks at Cody, and his heart begins to thud in his ears. There's a lot to tell, and she knows it all. The money he takes when nobody's looking. The foster home in Kanawha where the big boy liked to play "Baby,

baby." The night their mother left. "I'm going to tell your scoutmaster," she says.

His new father laughs, drapes an arm over his shoulders. "Boy Scouts aren't supposed to eat s'mores because the Girl Scouts invented them," he tells the other grown-ups. Then he pulls Cody into a head-lock, rubs his knuckles roughly across his head, whispers in Cody's ear. "We won't tell."

He knocks Beth's knee hard with his own. He looks up at the stars. He feels like making the excited sounds the loons make on the lake at night when they find one another out there in the dark. Beside him, Beth pouts, pushing sand into the fire with her heels until their new mother pats her knee and makes her stop. He pulls his charred marshmallow out of the fire, slides the burnt layer away and smears the gooey insides onto the Hershey bar, smashes the graham cracker on top and crams the whole sweet mess into his mouth. He eats three and then his new mother says, "Enough, Cody." She isn't smiling, but she isn't frowning either. She looks at him the way she does. "You're not fooling me, Cody," she says sometimes. "But I love you. I love you a lot." He knows he's supposed to say he loves her, too, and he guesses he does, but he can't.

The logs and sticks have fallen in and turned to pulsing coals that give off steady heat and an amber light that makes every person look like they're thinking deep thoughts. The heat warms his legs. Finally, his father gets up and adds another log so that sparks shower up, then flames sprout and run along the undersides of the wood.

"Let's tell stories," Mrs. Bradley says. "One time we saw the northern lights from this beach," she says, looking up at the sky. "They started as a green glow on the horizon over there, but before long there were fountains and sprays of light shooting all the way up to the top of the sky. Green, blue, red, it was unbelievable. We stayed out here until 2 or 3 in the morning. We couldn't stop watching. It was so cold we were shivering, but we wouldn't go in. We didn't want to miss a minute of it."

"I wish we could see them now," Beth says. "Do you think if we stay here all night, they might come out?"

"It could happen," she says, still looking up. "It just might. Let's watch for them," she says, and Beth crawls up into their new mother's lap and snuggles in like she belongs there.

Beth picks up her plastic horse and brushes him off. "This is Little Gray," she says. "He can jump over the moon."

The grown-ups look at each other and smile. He knows that smile. *Isn't she cute?* Their new mother leans over and kisses the top of her head. Beth is *so* stupid. She shouldn't ever let the grown-ups see how small and stupid she is. He nudges her in the side—their signal that she's being a baby—and she elbows him back, hard, in the ribs. "Stop it, Cody," their mother says. "That's a good story." She wraps her arms around his sister. She's still wearing the crown, and she's put on a green sweatshirt. Beth tips Little Gray at him. *Take that.* He snatches at the horse, but she's too quick. He'd throw the stupid thing in the fire if he could.

Beth has a dollhouse now, a scale-model stable full of palominos and bays and pinto ponies. He has a new rod and reel, a red down jacket and a mountain bike. If he has a bad dream, his new mother and father will both sit on his bed and talk to him, but he has nothing that their mother touched or picked out for him the way she chose Little Gray for Beth's 2nd birthday. Nothing he'd grabbed to take with him the way Beth had grabbed Little Gray from Jerry's recliner the morning the woman came to get them in the white car with the West Virginia state seal on both front doors. Nothing he can touch and feel close to her, and if he doesn't have anything to remember her by, Beth shouldn't either.

"Cody and Beth," his new mother says, "your Dad and I were driving down to Charleston to visit the Bradleys. We'd heard on the radio that tornadoes had been spotted in the area, but your dad wanted to go. You know how he is about traveling." She's trying to pull him in, reaching for him, but he looks up at the stars, and he feels like one of them, far away and cold, out there in the wilderness of the sky.

"We were driving down the highway through these open fields covered with corn stubble, and we were getting very nervous because the sky was green and the clouds had these funny tips hanging from them. Then, all of a sudden there's a tornado coming across the field. Not a big one, but big enough, and loud. They do sound just like trains bearing down on you, and we could see tree limbs and paper and corn shucks whirling around inside it. We could also see the path it was taking, and we knew that it was going to get to the road just about the time we did. I wanted to stop and get out and lie in a ditch like they tell you to do, but your Dad *sped up.* I couldn't believe it. The closer it got, the louder it roared, and we were yelling at each other about what to do, but we couldn't hear for the sound.

"And your Dad sped up again." She put a hand on his knee. "That tornado crossed the road right behind us. It bounced like a ball and came down in the field across the road and the dirt started flying. When we stopped up the road a little way, we were both shaking so hard our teeth were chattering. What were we thinking?" She laughs and shakes her head. They laugh together.

His Dad pokes at the fire. Sparks fly up and smoke twists away. "Your turn, Cody," he says. The fire snaps and across the fire, Mr. Bradley rubs his wife's arms. Beth's eyes look heavy as their new mother braids his sister's hair. He feels them waiting, and he wishes he had a story like theirs to tell. But he doesn't, and he has to say something. "One time my mom's boyfriend was beating her up. Jerry," he says. "He's her father." He nudges Beth with his elbow, but she doesn't jab him back. She's busy combing Little Gray's mane with her fingers, turning her head one way then another, her prissy way of letting him know she's not listening, but he knows she is.

What happened was that Jerry caught them in his chair one night. It had been dark when he and Beth curled up there and fell asleep, but when they woke up, it was gray outside and Jerry was screaming in his face. Then his mother was there, swaying over him, yanking him up off the floor where Jerry had pushed him. "I swear, Cody, why do you have to go and make him mad like that?" she said. Beth stood next to him with her thumb in her mouth. "Go on upstairs and take your sister with you," she said.

They're all looking into the fire now, and the fire's reflection ripples out across the water. His new father tries to pull him onto his lap, but he twists out from under his hand. He's found his mother, and he isn't going to lose her again. He tells them about the scream and the crash that shook the floor and made Beth whimper and cling to him. Then it got quiet. He tries to tell them about that quiet. How he lay on the mattress with Beth and listened to her breathe and studied the ice crystals on the window. How he listened for his mother's voice while the quiet went on and on. He tells them how he called the police and how they came and took Jerry away.

The day after that, he tells them, his mother wouldn't talk to him. She rocked in her chair and cried and drank from a bottle until it was empty and then she drove off in the rusty black truck with the busted tail light. Two days later, when she hadn't come back, he and Beth ate the last can of tomato soup, and then they walked across a field of frozen stubble to the neighbor's house. The lady in the white car came that afternoon and took them away with her.

Then they lived in a bunch of foster homes until their new mother and father adopted them.

"The End," he says, and he pokes his stick into the fire so hard sparks whirl up and fly away.

His new parents look at each other over his head. His new mother smooths his hair. In her arms, Beth's eyes droop, her fingers move slowly through Little Gray's mane, the way she does every night to put herself to sleep. Beth feels safe with these people who outran a tornado and he's glad. His new father shifts on the blanket, presses closer to him. He leans over to whisper in Cody's ear. "It's all right, Cody," he says, as though that's a secret.

Mrs. Bradley raises her glass. "Here's to all of you," she says. "To the good memories you're going to make together."

"I'll drink to that," his father says quietly.

"No, but listen," he says. Then he stops. "Never mind," he says. When he said, 'The End,' that wasn't true. He's left out the most important part. He hasn't told them how he ran downstairs and saw his mother lying on the floor like something broken. He won't tell them how Jerry knelt next to her saying, "Baby? Baby, wake up," or how he jumped on Jerry's back, meaning to kill him, the way Jerry had killed his first and only mother. He'll skip the part about how Jerry was choking him when his mother got up and grabbed a piece of wood from the pile beside the fireplace and hit Jerry across the face and knocked his nose sideways onto his cheek or how the blood jumped out through his fingers and turned his shirt red.

That's the best part of the story, the part he's keeping to himself. His mother got up from the floor that time, she can do it again. At this very moment, she might be getting up from another floor and making plans to come for him.

He shivers in the cool night air. His father puts an arm around his shoulder, draws him close. "Come here, son," he says. His shirt smells of the soap they wash clothes with back in the stone house on the hill near Parkersburg. He wishes he were there right now, going through pockets for the coins he's saving in case he needs to buy a bus ticket. But for now, he leans back against his new father's chest, lets the man wrap his jacket around him. It's as good a place as any to wait for her to come and take him home to the shelter.

Island

She slept most of the time now, and every day he sat beside the bed that hospice had set up in their room, waiting for her to wake up so he could talk to her. He knew they hadn't talked enough in the fifty-three years they'd been married, but they'd been so busy or it was never the right time. Then, after the surgery a few years ago, she'd wanted to show him the scar where her breast had been, but he couldn't look, and since he didn't know why, he'd walked out of the room while she was unbuttoning her blouse, and after that they'd hardly talked at all.

Well, he was sorry, but no matter what he'd done, it was wrong for her to leave him alone in this world when he'd felt alone for much, for *most,* of his life. Maybe if she understood that, she'd stay, and he would show her he could listen, too. She'd see they still needed each other, even though all she seemed to need from him now was another dose of morphine, or a few drops of water squeezed into her mouth from a small sponge.

He needed to tell her how the loneliness began one night while he was flounder gigging with his father and brother. Low tide on a moonless night was when we went after flounder he'd say. The tidal creeks were shallow then, my love, and with no moon to dazzle the water, a person with a flashlight could see clear to the bottom, where the flounder burrowed into the mud.

Those nights he stood in the bow of their faded green metal fishing boat with a gig cocked and ready, and his brother pointed a flashlight at the water. When he saw the outline of a flounder, he struck, then tossed the fish over his shoulder, got ready to stab again. He and his brother took turns in the bow with the light and the gig while their father steered the boat from a seat in the stern and cheered them on. Every time he tossed a fish over his shoulder the blood rained down, so that by the time the tide turned and the creeks rose and the fish disappeared beneath the murky water, everyone in the boat was spattered with blood.

One night there were so many flounder one gig could not spear them all, but it was dangerous to work two gigs in a small boat, so his father made a decision. They'd leave the younger boy—him—on one side of the island while his brother and father went around to the other. "Divide and conquer," their father said.

"Worked for Custer," the boy said, collecting his gear, resigned. He was twelve that summer. He loved the great battles—Little Big Horn, Gettysburg, Waterloo—where everything was won or lost.

His father poked his older brother in the shoulder. "Help me remember to come back for him, will you?" he said. Their father loved practical jokes. In a shop that sold magic tricks, he'd bought a little pink rubber pig with plug in the belly, like a saltshaker. He'd catch a few flies and put them into the pig, then set it on the table before a meal. The first Sunday the pig appeared on the table, the boy saw its ear twitch, then its tail, heard a faint buzz. He couldn't believe it so he watched and listened until the pig twitched again. Then he said, "See that? It moved. Everybody watch."

His father felt his forehead. "I'm worried about you, Cooch," he said. The family laughed and the boy laughed along with them. It felt good to be teased a little and called by the nickname his father had given him. The trouble was, his father didn't know when to stop. He'd teased the boy about the pig until tears stood in his eyes and he'd started to believe that he might really *be* the gullible baby his father seemed to think he was, the runt of the litter of three sisters and a brother, who all agreed with their father: the pig didn't twitch or buzz, Cooch is just making things up.

Imagine, he wanted to say to his wife, how it felt to climb out of the boat onto the beach with a gig, a bucket and a light and watch your father and brother shove the boat back into the surf. He could see his father now, and he wanted her to see him, too, jumping back into the boat with his pants rolled up to his knees, his legs flashing white in the dark water.

"Go get 'em, Cooch," he said, as he yanked the rope and started the outboard engine. "We'll be back."

He walked over the dunes to a tidal creek and sloshed along in his rubber boots, scanning the bottom for fish, using the light his father had rigged onto the front of his wide-brimmed canvas hat. That night, he stumbled into flounder heaven. He worked his gig so fast, he might have been shoveling the fish while the blood rained down on his hat and jacket.

When the bucket was full, he carried it back to the beach and squatted on the sand and watched the waves break while he waited for his father and brother. He listened for the sound of the outboard motor but all he heard was the boom and swish of surf, the rasp of palmettoes. Overhead, he saw the stars and the long gauzy brightness of the Milky Way.

He waited for as long as it should have taken them to come back, and then he closed his eyes and tried to remember his father buttoning his jacket, squaring it on his shoulders. Instead, he remembered the little pink pig on the white tablecloth and the way his father had laughed when he'd insisted it had twitched, because his father thought it was funny to tease people until they doubted what they'd seen or heard. But leaving your son alone on an island at night was different from teasing him about a trick-shop pig on the Sunday dinner table. Sometimes, though, his father didn't seem to know the difference, and that frightened him.

Then the thought of himself as a person a father could forget frightened him even more and he felt how small and insignificant he was, like a shell you picked up on the beach, then dropped when you got bored with it. When he finally heard the motor, he ran back into the dunes and squatted there, hugging his knees. The prow of the boat rasped across the sand.

"Cooch?" his father called. No answer.

"COOCH." A command. Not to come now was defiance, but he kept himself quiet by imagining himself small and cold and forgotten.

His father's flashlight swept the beach, paused at the bucket of fish, moved on. "Godamnit, Cooch, where are you?"

He let the ocean answer and the silence of the stars. He waited and he listened while his father called and called for him. He didn't know what he was listening for, but when he heard in his father's voice that *he* felt small and frightened, too, the boy stood up and walked out of the dunes.

"Here I am," he said.

The loneliness began that night, he wanted to tell her. And it stayed. During the war, he fought in New Guinea and the Philippines, all the way to the edge of Japan. She'd written to him every day, and he hadn't thanked her for that, so he thanked her now. Folded inside her letters were drawings of the house they'd build when he came home and photographs of herself in a new hat, or squares of cloth cut with pinking shears from a dress she was making. She signed each letter with *Take care of you for me,* as though her well-being depended on his. They'd been married for five months when he left for the Pacific. How many children do you want? They wrote to one another. Three, she'd say, and he'd say why not four? By the end of the war the count was up to a dozen.

He needed to tell her that he'd read every letter. He'd studied the drawings and imagined their house, this house. He'd touched the cloth and tried to take care of himself for her, for them. But mostly, he'd hunkered in a foxhole at night in the rain. When the rain pattered on his helmet and dripped from it and slid down his neck, the old loneliness returned. He was abandoned on the beach again, no one was coming back for him.

On one of those desolate foxhole nights, someone tapped him on the shoulder and he looked up at another soldier's tired face and dripping helmet.

"Got a hot meal for you, Captain," the other man said. He reached up and took the tin plate, and the warmth of it startled him.

He wanted to tell her about that moment, so she could feel the warmth of the plate and see the man's kind face. He wanted her to know that their life together had made him as grateful as he felt that night, far from home in the rain. He was sorry, he'd tell her, he was ashamed that he hadn't been able to look at her scar. The war had something to do with that failure, but he still couldn't find the why of it.

He sat beside her bed for a week, rehearsing the things he wanted to tell her, and then the hospice nurse said it was time to call the children. When he'd done that, he went back and sat by her bed and thought again about being alone on this earth. Saying those words to himself, he felt angry, as though some promise had been broken.

The night before the children came, a thunderstorm blew in. The wind rose, kept rising, lightning struck almost continuously. The thunder sounded like the guns on the Navy ships, shelling the beach before the infantry landed, and he remembered churning toward the beach on a landing craft and realizing he'd forgotten to tell his men to lock and load and now the Navy guns were too loud for them to hear him.

After the storm blew the power out, he groped across the room to the closet and took down the battery-powered lantern that he kept there for emergencies. He switched on the light and stood beside her bed so that she wouldn't wake alone in the dark and remember she was dying. But she didn't stir or wake; the morphine carried her through the night.

In the morning, as he did every morning now, he stood at the foot of the bed, where she could see him. This was the moment he dreaded most, when she studied him until she knew him, and every day he waited longer for her to remember who he was. But on the morning after the storm, her eyes were as bright and sly as the eyes of a child with a secret. He took her hand. "What do you need?" he said.

"Who were you fighting?" she whispered. "You were really fighting them." Then she drifted back to sleep.

Her words flooded through him like warm oil. Last night, he'd been alone in the foxhole with death all around. He'd been a boy left alone on an island. Yet from deep in her drugged sleep, she'd fought her way back to him; she'd come through the storm to say she'd heard him, and at least for that moment, neither of them was alone.

Forward, Elsewhere, Out

1

A rainy night in early October, her favorite time of day and year, her favorite weather. She's never told anyone, not even her husband Thomas, how these dreary nights make the house feel like a refuge, an outpost on the edge of a cold, rainy wilderness that begins just outside the door and goes on from there, forever. When the children were small, she'd left the kitchen door cracked open to let in the sound, hoping they'd hear.

Tonight, out of habit, she's opened the back door a crack, but she and Eli, the youngest, are the only two sheltering here. Thomas is rocketing around Japan on a high-speed train, negotiating a big contract for his most important client. Kate, her namesake daughter, is studying art history in Florence this semester. She is stirring a pot of chili when Eli jumps up to sit on the counter beside the stove, the way he does when he wants to talk—they've always been close. "How are you this fine, rainy evening?" she says.

He watches her steadily through his hazel eyes, dark hair flopped down on his forehead, a shadow of hair on his upper lip. A line from a song drifts through her mind: *Eli's coming, hide your heart, girl.* "You know, Mother," he says. "What Rachel and I do is our business."

She can guess what business they mean to transact, but she keeps stirring the chili, staying calm. "Interesting," she says, marking her place in the conversation while she waits for a better answer to come to her.

In another time, when he wasn't sixteen and she was still his pal, his *Mom,* she might have tried for a joke, but she's stung by the new formality of *Mother,* and by the ambush, as if he's just made a surprise move in a long chess match.

Which, come to think of it, he has. This match, to keep Eli from learning what he's determined to find out, has been going on since he'd turned secretive and short-tempered at thirteen, and her brother had urged them to break into Eli's internet history.

Sure enough, they'd found a few items there to paste in the scrapbook of twenty-first century childhood: first trip to a porn website, first chat room conversation. They hadn't made a big deal about it; they'd moved the computer out of his room and into the den for a few months, then she and Thomas had sat down and talked with Eli about the dangers of chatting with anonymous strangers, the ugly distortions of pornography. They bought him a book, *It's Perfectly Natural,* a collection of line drawings of young people exploring their bodies, liking what they saw and felt. He kept it in a duffel bag under his bed, along with a *Sports Illustrated* swimsuit issue he'd gotten from somewhere, as if, even though they'd bought the book for him, he still needed to hide it from them.

She takes a deep breath, moves the spoon through the chili in a slow figure-eight. "Well, of course it's your *business,* Eli," she says, stepping carefully from word to word. "Dad and I can't be your conscience." He ducks his head to hide a smile, and who can blame him? *Conscience.* A prissy old word like that deserves a smirk. It conjures up her grandmother's parlor; it nudges Jimminy Cricket onto the stage to sing his brave little song: *always let your conscience be your guide.*

She remembers laughing with her women friends about how much they loved their baby boys and the pleasure of being adored with such pure passion. She remembers the open eagerness of Eli's eyes, which seemed to register every ripple in his soul; she remembers holding him and feeling that her full share of life's happiness lay sleeping in her arms. "Paging Dr. Freud. Why don't we just name them all *Oedipus* and get it over with?" she'd said to her friends when Eli was almost two and she was the last one still nursing, a choice, her friends told her, that only the La Leche League would support. Now her friends are grieving that their sons have clammed up on them. *At least he's still talking to me,* she thinks, staring into the chili, swirling it slowly with the lopsided wooden spoon that Eli had hacked and sanded for her one year at summer camp.

But it is time to face facts. Rachel has her driver's license, not just a learner's permit, like Eli. She can drive anywhere, anytime. At this moment, she is driving here in her silver Honda to carry Eli away with her to the dead end streets and vacant lots that everyone's children know the way to. She remembers those places herself. A dirt road overlooking a quarry where she and her college boy-friend went to make out. The house of a friend whose parents were out of town where they'd spent their first night in bed together. Which reminds her that someone's parents are *always* out of town.

"How about talking to Dad?" she says.

"Who?" He shrugs, looks away, mouth tightening, drums his heels against the cabinet door.

She knows their son's opinion of Thomas's latest trip to Japan, his third this year. In the saucepan, the chili bubbles thickly. She takes another deep breath, stirs it down and hurries on. "Well, you're too young, Eli, you really are. Both of you. At least talk to Dad about it."

Eli flinches, then he recovers and looks back at her with a touch of what—amusement?—in his eyes. *A talk?* he seems to say. *You want me to talk with Dad about sex? Do old people even have sex? When was the last time anyone thought of sex as a mystery that sons were ushered into by their fathers? And did she really just say it?* Doing *it.* She's always hated that phrase, but making love sounds too hushed and precious for these loud, crude times. No, it is the right word for what the men and women were doing to one another on the websites Eli had visited. For what she sees everyday on laptops quickly shut as she patrols the aisles between the long tables in the middle school library where she's in charge, but not really. On papers retrieved between classes from under those tables. Just this week, she found a much-handled picture of a naked girl straddling a mirror, her breasts with their pierced nipples thrust forward.

He checks his watch, jumps down the from counter. "OK, later," he says.

"No supper, Eli?" she says. "I made this for you." Chili and cornbread when the weather turns cool, his favorite meal.

"Gotta go," he kisses her on the top of her head, pats her shoulder.

She shrugs him off. "OK," she says, managing her voice. "Be careful on the road. Tell Rachel she needs to slow down when it rains. The tires don't . . . "

" . . . grip the pavement as well when there's water on the road," he finishes for her.

"You've got money?"

"I've got money."

"Midnight, Eli," she says. "Think about what I said."

"By your leave, my lady mother," he says, bowing deeply, then swoops in to kiss her loudly on the cheek.

"Be gone," she says, waving him away with the spoon.

The front door closes, locks, and she is alone in the wilderness outpost, stirring her chili, while the cold rain splashes onto the brick patio outside the kitchen door. The first time Thomas called from Japan, he told her about flying over the Arctic circle. He watched the trees thin out and disappear, then they flew for hours over the polar ice cap. "You can't believe how much nothing there is up there," he said. Now, as she eats a bowl of chili at the kitchen table, the newspaper folded and propped on the sugar bowl in front of her, she feels like she is the one flying alone over the empty vastness at the top of the world.

But there's still hope. At least Eli's not with the girl up the street, the one in the tank top and low-slung jeans, her eyes as darkly lined as a goddess from an Egyptian tomb, who'd knocked on their door the day after her family moved into the neighborhood last fall and asked for Eli by name. Eli is with Rachel, sweet, serious Honor Society Rachel, in her pressed jeans and polo shirt, and the pastel butterfly barrettes holding back her light blonde hair. Rachel who *volunteers* to wash dishes, then scrubs the glasses, inside and out, and washes the bottoms of plates, while Eli clowns around the kitchen, doing tricks with the dishtowel and drying the dishes she hands him. They are such children still.

2.

At one a.m. the front door bangs open and Eli heads straight for the refrigerator. He rummages there, assembles something with much rustling and ripping, a clatter of ice cubes into a glass, carries the plate and glass into the dining room and flops down at his place at the table. She watches him from the couch in the darkened den just off the kitchen, where she's waited since midnight, clipping loose threads off of her chenille bathrobe and steadily aging, until by the time he comes in, she feels like some ancient creature brooding in its lair. Finally she stands up from the couch, cinches the bathrobe tighter, because when rules are broken, someone must take charge, and she is the only grown-up here. She leans on the dining room doorjamb with her arms folded, waiting, until Eli looks up from his plate.

"Evening, Mother," he says around a mouthful of sandwich, and she notes that his hair has recently been *combed*. Such a detective she's become.

"You're late," she says, stops herself from saying *Mister*, like a 50's Mom. He nods, shrugs. "Sorry," he says, frowning at the sandwich.

She waits for the excuse, something to show that the rules still matter here, and he knows he's broken one. Instead, the cell phone beside his plate rings, and he holds up a finger, *just a second,* as though he hates to interrupt, but he has to take this call. He answers the phone, then turns away, but not before she sees a smile spread across his face.

She knows that smile, the one that isn't yours to start or stop, the one that turns your face into a movie screen where happiness is now playing. If you're lucky, you get to smile like that, hostage to joy, a few times in your life. She remembers smiling at Thomas on their wedding day, smiling helplessly at each newborn child. Before she can say more, Eli gets up from the table and walks out the back door into the yard. The rain has stopped, and under the dripping backyard oak, Eli paces and talks and smiles. She imagines that he's about to start dancing, and she turns away, a spasm gripping her heart that *can't* be jealousy, it can't be, but it is.

Patience, she tells herself all the next day. Watch and wait. She *will* talk to Eli, she must. Like the happiness that spills into a smile, this need to talk, to teach, to *matter* will not be denied, it's an occupational hazard of motherhood. But timing is everything, so she waits until the next evening, when they're driving to pick up take-out from their favorite Chinese restaurant. She drives, and Eli lounges against the passenger-side door, doodling swirls and spirals on the fogged up glass, then erasing them with a swipe of his shirtsleeve. Ten minutes into the drive, his cell phone has rung twice, and he's had two happy conversations. "Yep, sure am. Definitely. Not much longer. OK. OK, bye."

While he talks on the phone, she rehearses her speech, but every sentence she tries out sounds like the Old Testament God thundering at his shivering creatures when he caught on to what they'd been up to in his garden. *Who told thee thou wast naked?* Why did you open your eyes when I would have kept you blind and happy as puppies forever?

Finally, after he snaps his phone shut for the second time, when she figures she has a minute, two minutes, tops, before the phone rings again, she says, "The thing is, Eli, I just don't want you and Rachel opening that door." She could have smacked herself in the forehead for that one.

He looks at her as though he'd expected her to say something like that, as though she's become as transparent to him as he once was to her, all her little feints and dodges. He reaches across the seat, pats her arm. "Mom, don't worry," he says, placating her with the *Mom.* "I'm not a horn-dog."

"Well, that's reassuring," she says, while her inner grandmother, whose stuffy parlor they'd visited earlier for a lecture on *conscience,* explodes in righteous fury. *Don't talk filth to me, boy,* she says.

If only she had her grandmother's words, or the words from her old Catholic Girls Manual to deploy with Eli, words to keep him close, or at least too scared to disobey, the way she'd been. She'd spent eight years in Catholic school, steeped in the language of chastity and sin. When a boy whistled at her on the first day of ninth grade in public school, she ran and hid behind a tree. Her Christian brother still has that grip on his teenage daughter, or he *thinks* he does. She's vowed to keep her virginity until marriage and she wears a promise ring, a white gold band set with crosses, *Love Waits* engraved inside the band. But those words and promises, the faith her brother puts in faith, seem flimsy in the age of horn-dogs and pierced girls and their mirrors.

Later, after a silent dinner eaten out of cartons in front of the TV, Eli departs for his upstairs bedroom and she goes into the kitchen, where she wipes the counters and watches the clock and waits for Thomas to call. What she really wants right now is the man himself. She wants to lie down with him on their big bed in the dark and touch his face and hear him tell her not to be sad. She wants to hear *Thomas's* story again, the story of the only child who became his mother's little man after his father left them. And yet, he will say, when the time came, his mother packed him off to college and let him go out into the world, where he found a wife and children to love and went on loving his mother, too, giving back to her what she'd been willing to let him go away from her to find.

Tonight she will have to settle for his voice. Exactly at eight, the phone rings, and she brings Thomas up to speed on the news from this side of the world: the missed curfew, the combed hair. "What should I do?" she whispers. He's quiet for a few seconds, and she rests in his silence, waiting. Then in his calm, reasonable way, he says, "I wish I was there with you."

The simple kindness of those words throws a switch and the words pour out. She tells him how old and weird she feels, whispering to him in Japan about how carefully their son has combed his hair. She tells him about the brooding creature she turned into the night she waited up for Eli. The euphemisms she blew like bubbles in the car on the way to the restaurant. If Thomas were here, they would laugh about her dark scenarios, and the laughter would lighten the darkness. Thomas, the only person on the whirling planet to whom she can tell this nightmare fairy tale in which she stars as the hag brooding darkly over the world that their son is launching himself so eagerly out into.

She feels like a warden, she tells him, a guard patrolling the prison of safety and home that must be escaped for the new life of freedom and possibility. And sex. "Let's not forget sex," she says.

"Who wants to?" Thomas says. "Let me speak to him."

While they talk, Eli paces in the upstairs hall, and she stays in the kitchen with the radio on so she can't hear, but when he hands the phone back to her, she senses that no advice was offered from far Japan and none will be, except to her. "Relax," Thomas says. In his voice, she hears a residue of laughter. Have they been joking about this? "You can't change anything. They'll be all right. Remember that carrot and condom drill they did in sex-ed class?"

"I'd rather not," she says. "Hurry home."

"I'm on my way."

3.

The night after the conversation with his father that changes exactly nothing, Eli hops up onto the counter beside the stove again while she cooks spaghetti, another favorite meal. She is *not* doing this to keep him home, away from Rachel. No. Rachel's been invited to her house for dinner because Eli's mother is an open-minded woman who accepts the world as it is—piercings, mirrors and all. She looks forward to having Rachel at their table, where she will keep up her end of the conversation, then stand at the sink, with the little blue butterflies holding back her blonde hair, and wash the dishes and the glasses inside and out, same as always.

She's about to ask Eli to set the table when he glances at his watch, the way people do when they can't wait to leave. Is that what's happening here? He wants to escape? He does, but she's the one who's making this personal, and in her more serene moments she knows that. Something like the movement of tides, the push of seasons, the urgency of birth itself, is carrying him away. He's going where every cloud, leaf, seed, every man, woman and child goes: forward, elsewhere, onward, out. He's not leaving *her* anymore than he left *her* when he was born, and what is needed here is what every birth requires— surrender. Surrender and maybe a ceremony to mark ends and beginnings, the way women in India give away one precious object every year, to practice letting go. Thomas says that in Japan, when a bullet train pulls into a station, the attendants line up and bow, as though the train were a god, the god of speed and change. Maybe she should bow to Eli, then let him speed away.

"What's the hurry, Eli?" she asks.

"Rachel's picking me up at 7. We'll grab something to eat before the movie."

"I thought you all were having supper here," she says. She raps the spoon hard on the rim of the pot, and sauce flies up and splatters on the stove.

"I'm sorry, Mom," he says, "I'm sorry, I forgot." His shoulders slump, and he sounds like a little boy again, the one who took every mistake to heart, gave his parents hand-colored cards of apology and remorse.

"It's all right, Eli," she says. "Everybody forgets, but you know, I just don't want either one of you to get hurt," she hurries on, knowing she shouldn't, but like the smile that will be smiled, it can't be stopped: "And what if Rachel gets pregnant," she says. "Have you thought about that?"

"Mother, please," he says. His eyes dart around the room, trapped. "Don't make me sorry I talked to you in the first place."

That threat brings tears to her eyes, and once they're there, she can feel a river of tears rising, rushing through the hole made by the arrow he's fired straight through her heart. They've always talked; now he's threatening to take that away as she makes this rough shift from Mom, playmate, buddy, to Mother, spy, unwelcome guest. He doesn't need to leave his father; Thomas lives in the world of men where Eli wants to go, out where motherhood is not a woman's highest calling. And this is only his first departure.

"Don't be late," she calls after him.

"Word," he says, and slams the front door behind him.

4.

He comes in after one again, ignores her where she sits in the den, watching a movie. He rummages through the pantry and refrigerator, then comes into the den carrying a bowl of cereal and sits down on the edge of the cushions at the far end of the couch, not looking at her. *Late Marriage* is the name of the movie, an Israeli film. She'd expected a comedy, which it's not, but now she's involved in the story, and she wants to know how it will turn out. The movie is about a family that's desperate to get their son married. He's almost forty, still a bachelor, and the worry is that he will always be. But he will not marry any of the women his mother and father choose for him because he's secretly involved with a divorced woman. When his family finds out, there's a terrible scene. Mother, father, uncles crowd into the woman's apartment and demand that she give him up. An uncle even threatens the woman with a sword, but she stands up to the man's family, even though he can't. When Eli comes in, the family is gone, and the movie couple is cleaning up the mess.

"What's this about?" he says, still not looking at her, spooning cereal into his mouth. She glances over at him. He hasn't bothered to comb his hair, as if it doesn't matter anymore what she knows.

"A man whose family doesn't want him to be with the person he's with," she says, and sees the secret smile begin on his face, *Oh, that story.* As though he knows them all now. "They're trying to stop him from seeing her, but he won't."

"Is it any good?" he says. She can feel him trying to be buddies again, the way they used to be. Settling in with a bowl of popcorn between them to watch an episode of *Jackass.* Laughing together at the idiotic boys who rode their bicycles full-speed into thorny hedges, then backed up and did it again.

"It's all right," she says. "Darker than I'd expected, though."

And then, suddenly, the couple in the movie falls onto the bed. If she'd seen it coming, she would have switched off the TV, but it happened too fast, and now she can't move. The sex on the screen is not like the usual movie sex, lush music and firelight playing over a tangle of soft-focus bodies. This scene plays out in a room lit harshly by an overhead light, on a bed with rumpled white sheets where two people begin to kiss and touch and struggle out of their clothes.

She waits for the lights to dim, for the camera to look away, but it continues to stare. Eli stops crunching his cereal. He sits completely still, his face turning red. She wishes she could say *something* to help him understand what he's seeing, the way she did when they watched the Titanic go down or saw Frodo lose the ring. And then it comes to her, she sees it as clearly as if the movie she's watching is about her and her son.

In this scene, the boy's not leaving after all. In fact he's stepped right into her world, and even though they live in the same world now, *because* they do, it's forbidden that they talk to each other about what they both know. From now on, like everyone else in this fallen world, they will surround themselves with widening circles of privacy, with the borders clearly marked to discourage trespassing. He stands up, cereal bowl in one hand, wipes the other down the side of his jeans. "I know what you're thinking," he says.

It takes her a few seconds to understand that he's accusing her of picturing him and Rachel as the couple on the bed. She almost laughs when she realizes she's never imagined that scene, not even once. She's pacing off the first few yards of her own distance now. "Actually, son," she says, "you don't."

Rich

Now that Nathan had moved out, Lucille was free to live as she pleased. Today it pleased her to put on her green silk kimono and drink a cup of dark roast coffee at the kitchen table while she listened to Segovia romance the guitar. It wasn't that she didn't love her son, and she'd loved his father, too, her ex-husband Peter, but life felt so much less cluttered and complicated, so much more *spacious,* without them. Yesterday she'd hung a new, framed poster on the wall next to the refrigerator. *Simplify. Simplify. A man is rich in proportion to the number of things which he can afford to let alone.* Thoreau's words floated in empty white space.

At fifty she was making steady progress toward that goal. She was thinner than she'd been in years, wore long earrings and short skirts again. When she looked in the mirror she wasn't exactly *pleased*—what woman ever is?—but she wasn't depressed either. Thanks to Peter's alimony check and a small inheritance from her parents, carefully managed, she didn't have to work; she could spend her time growing rich in Thoreau's way.

Nathan had graduated from high school in May, and in June he announced that he was deferring admission to the state university in order to live in what he called *the real world* for a year. "Fine with me," she said after he sketched his plan to move into an apartment and work at Nuts and Berries, a local health food store. "Go, fly, I love you," she said, surprised at how easy it had been to let him go, how relieved she'd felt, if she were being completely honest with herself.

Nathan had taken so much with him when he left. His hair care products, for instance, that had lined the shelves and overflowed the counters of the single, small bathroom the three of them had shared. He'd been growing his hair since his thirteenth birthday, and he lavished every tenderness on it. Shampoos, conditioners, pomades, he'd arranged them all by type and size, from tall squeeze bottles down to one, small, cobalt-blue jar of a fragrant, clear gel called *Brilliant* that he combed through his hair before a date or a holiday dinner.

The TV was gone, too, a gift she'd insisted he take. They'd bickered about it the whole time he packed. "You need a TV," she said. "I don't."

"But what will you do without it?" he'd asked, his dark, sad eyes looking out from the parted curtains of his lank hair, his thin shoulders drooping. He'd always been stubbornly bony. Chicken and dumplings had been his favorite food, but no matter how many helpings she'd spooned onto his plate, he'd stayed thin, as though his body refused nourishment.

"I'll read a book. I'll watch the seasons turn. It doesn't take much to make me happy," she said.

He'd rolled his eyes and walked away, but she'd had the last word. The morning he moved out he was stuffing the last load of clothes into the backseat of his black Toyota Corolla when she'd carried the TV down the front steps and shoved it in on top of the heap. "You'll be doing me a favor," she said.

That morning she'd waved from the porch, walked back into the house and sat on the living room sofa for a while, enjoying the silence. Nathan had taken his noise with him, too. One more complication gone. After Peter left for New Orleans, their son started going into his room at night and listening to the heavy-metal music his father had loathed and forbidden. The music sounded like a train wreck punctuated by obscenities and the screams of the dying, and he played it so loud it throbbed in the floor joists and rafters and rolled through the house like a menacing current.

Let him have it, she thought for the first three months. This must be the soundtrack of his inner life, a passing storm of grief for his father. But the music kept playing. From the day Peter left until the day two years later when Nathan moved out, he played his music every night. One night as she hurried toward her room with her hands pressed over her ears, she found his bedroom door ajar. She peeked in, expecting to see his clothes ripped, his hair tangled by the violence of the sound. Instead, while the music fell on him like a collapsing building, he sat on the edge of his bed like a monk at prayer, with his hands clasped tightly between his knees, his eyes squeezed shut, his face lifted to the noise and chaos.

Now that the house was quiet, clean and calm, she could get serious about simplifying her life. Today, she and her friend Agnes would take their morning walk in the nature preserve outside of town. After lunch, she would go to Nuts and Berries to treat Nathan to a cup of coffee and a muffin. From the store she would go to the Y and wash away the day's grubbiness in the whirlpool, then home to a light supper of stir fried vegetables and rice and to bed by 9:30. She liked how it felt to live lightly on the face of the burdened earth. She locked the door behind her and stepped out into the morning, feeling light and free.

She met Agnes last June, at a divorce support group at St. Matthew's Episcopal Church, right after Agnes's husband, Richard, left her for a twenty-nine-year-old Mexican stripper with two small children, whom he'd met in Dallas while traveling on business. In April, Agnes found credit card receipts from the club where she worked, and Richard had confessed. In late May, he stuffed some clothes in a duffle bag and flew to Dallas to stay.

The summer after Richard left, she and Agnes walked every morning early, before the sky turned white and the humid heat hung over everything like smoke. North Carolina was the upper south, but it was still the south, where summer lasts. They walked as the trees turned red and orange and gold and the sky turned brilliant blue. When winter came, they walked through the snow in their lug-soled boots and down parkas. They walked while ice showered down from the bare trees and littered the frozen ruts in the road.

Now, it was spring, two years since Peter left, almost one year since Agnes had been deserted, but time was carrying them both. It was the closest she came to faith in anything, now. Faith in time. Time like an arrow, flying true. Like a boat under sail. A road through the wilderness. For a year after Peter left, she'd walked through a tunnel of grief. Keep moving was what she knew, and sooner or later, you'll walk out into the light. Agnes was still in the middle of the tunnel, walking blindly through the darkness and Louise was there to carry the flashlight. It was the least she could do.

Not that Peter was like Richard, a man who panicked in middle age at the prospect of getting old with the woman he'd once been young with. Who couldn't bear the way she sat across from him at the dinner table like death itself, stirring Metamucil into a glass of warm water, telling the same story for the hundredth time. There had been no other woman, no slashing blow to the heart to leave her wounded and bitter. The break-up of their marriage had been cleaner. One night after he washed and she dried the dishes, he draped the towel over the dish drainer the way she liked it done. "Sit down with me, Lucille," he said.

She remembered his dark beard sprinkled with gray, the red Peruvian cap with the ear flaps that he wore all winter because they kept the house at sixty-two degrees, to do their part in relieving the planet of the demands of its greedy human cargo. She remembered the sadness in his warm brown eyes when he took her hand and ran his thumb across her knuckles. "I cannot possibly be the man you want me to be," he said, "and I can't stand to fail at it any longer."

In their twenty years together she'd doubted his driving ability, his penny-pinching, his laissez-faire attitude toward their son, but she'd never questioned his sincerity, so when he said that, something grabbed her by the throat and the room dropped into darkness.

When she could see and talk again, she said, "Is it the thing about Paris, Peter? That's getting tiresome, isn't it?" Lucille had read in a biography of Dorothea Lange that the famous photographer called her husband *not a Paris kind of person.* Lucille had found that hilarious, and whenever Peter had tried to play a Pete Fountain tape, she'd say, "That is not the music of a Paris kind of person." Or "A Paris kind of person does not leave his dirty socks in the middle of the living room floor." For years, they'd both laughed at the joke, and then for more years, she was the only one who found it funny.

"It's not the thing about Paris," he said, and he looked at her steadily. He was moving to New Orleans, where he'd found a job as a city planner and there were plenty of clubs where he could sit in on clarinet at a Dixieland jazz session. They held each other for a long time that night. It was the closest they'd been in months.

When Lucille turned into the nature center parking lot, Agnes pushed off from the gray Honda station wagon she'd been leaning against and waved both arms above her head as though she were flagging down a train. "I'm right here, honey," Lucille said to herself as she parked next to Agnes. "I haven't gone anywhere." Was Agnes feeling desperate today? Clogged with despair? She took a quick inventory. Agnes had red hair and pale blue eyes, a milky, redhead's complexion. When she was sad, which she'd been for most of the last year, her nose sharpened, and her eyes looked weak; her face turned pinched and bloodless. But this morning, in a pale-green scarf and lipstick, Agnes looked happy. This was progress. They stretched their hamstrings and started walking down the long, straight dirt track through the woods. Water in the roadside ditches reflected a pale blue sky; the peepers were singing and on the highest branches new leaves hung in the air like green mist. "Tell me, tell me," Lucille said.

"Oh, Lu-Lu," Agnes said. "Maisie's back, and guess what?" Maisie was Agnes and Richard's seventeen year-old daughter. She blamed Agnes for the fact that her father had left them.

"What?" Lucille said.

"She *gets* it," Agnes said. "Maisie finally gets it."

Richard and Clarice had recently produced a baby boy named Tristan, and Maisie had flown to Dallas to meet her stepmother and new stepbrother. At the airport, Clarice marched up to Maisie and hugged her tight. Meanwhile, out in the concourse, her father waved and kept talking on his cell phone. Clarice was tall and thin, black hair skinned back into a knot. She was dressed in a black shirt, tight white Capri pants and high heeled shoes, a Prada bag slung over her shoulder, half a dozen gold bracelets (including a gold snake with a ruby eye) jingling on her wrists. Maisie had told Agnes all about it. Their idea of all of them getting to know each other was to leave Maisie with her new brother on Friday night while they took Clarice's two older children out to the movies. On Saturday night they parked the older children with their separate fathers and left the baby with her again. Close to midnight, he finally screamed himself to sleep, and when they came in at 3, Clarice teetered into the baby's room on her stiletto heels and made a big show of tugging the blue blanket up under his fat little chin.

"A gold snake with a ruby eye," Agnes said. "Is that perfect?" Her breathing came fast and shallow. Lucille squeezed her friend's arm, felt it tremble through her coat sleeve. Poor Agnes, she thought, still picking through the rubble.

"Breathe, Agnes," she said. "Maisie figured it out, didn't she? And so will you. Clarity comes, Aggie," she said. "Peace, too. You'll see."

Agnes laughed. "I'm trying to believe you," she said. "I really am." Fists jammed down into the pockets of her barn coat Agnes walked so fast Lucille had to trot to keep up with her. *At last, at last, at last,* their footsteps said.

When the doors of Nuts and Berries slid open, all the wind chimes rang. Music drifted through the air, something with strings, not really a melody, more like a cloud of music. She spotted her son immediately. His hair was held back with a green twist tie, and he was chatting with the man whose groceries he was bagging and he was *smiling.* She felt her shoulders relax. If she was being completely honest with herself, (and didn't telling the truth always simplify your life?) she went to the store to check on him. He always seemed glad to see her, or maybe *relieved* was more of what he seemed, the way he'd looked when she'd walked into his preschool at the end of the day, and he'd abandon the big plastic beads he'd been chewing on or jump up from the tiny table where he'd been drinking juice with the other toddlers and run to her and press his face between her legs as though she'd just rescued him from danger.

He'd only been working at the store for three weeks, and already he'd gotten two warnings: one for rudeness to a customer, the other for violating the dress code by coming to work in a black t-shirt with the words *If I throw a stick, will you leave?* printed across the front. Black clothing was prohibited at Nuts and Berries, his team leader told him. Only plain shirts in earth tones or neutral colors, or the green company shirt, were permissible work attire, she said, but it was the implied hostility of the message on Nathan's shirt that had troubled his team leader most. The message was clearly antisocial, and it was especially offensive to women, he'd been told, who had been victimized by language throughout history and were more vulnerable to name calling than men. Their mission, the team leader reminded him, was to create a safe and positive environment. Surely he could agree that wearing a black t-shirt with a hostile message on it was anything but positive. When he disagreed, she wrote him up. One more warning and he'd be let go.

Today, however, he was cheerful and now that she'd seen him looking cheerful, she could enjoy walking around the store while she waited for him to take his break. The store was large and full of light, the windowsills lined with flowers in pots and twisted bamboo stems set in vases filled with clear glass beads. The lasagna in the café steam table, the stuffed portobello mushrooms, brown rice, big urns of coffee and racks of muffins, breathed their fragrance into the air. She walked past the flowers and produce and then up and down each aisle, enjoying the sight and smell of the food, admiring the skill of the workers at the sushi bar who deftly wrapped seaweed around rice and tucked small pieces of fish into the center of each round. In the deli department, she fetched a toothpick from a small metal cup and speared three cubes of the organic baby Gouda from a blue plate. She grabbed a few crackers from a sample platter and circled back for another cheese cube.

Usually, it cheered her up to walk around the store. It was like wandering through a perfect world where no one was ever hungry or sad or lonely.

But today, it made her uneasy, and she couldn't shake the idea that in this universe of food and flowers, hunger was obscene, the un-beautiful were not welcome.

She looked at her watch. Almost time for Nathan's break. She walked up the pasta aisle and through the shelves of vitamins toward the cashier's station where her son was bagging groceries. He lifted the last bag into a woman's cart, then turned to the girl at the cash register. She was a pretty girl with light crinkled hair. A few steps closer, and she saw the girls' flushed face, the way she stood with her back against the counter next to the cash register and stared out the front window, smiling in a fixed kind of way. She edged closer, but her son hadn't seen her yet, he was entirely intent on the girl.

You're standing too close, she thought uneasily.

Lucille hesitated; another two steps and she would be able to hear what he was saying. Over the speakers, a woman's voice sang softly, accompanied by the breathing and sighing of strings, the music of a distant, beautiful world where her son wasn't making a pretty girl nervous.

Lucille stepped up behind the magazine rack at the entrance to the check-out line, studying the shelves of slippery elm lozenges, organic chocolate bars, packets of Vitamin C powder, as though she'd come there for something. "I'm talking about a real conversation here, Myra," he said. "I mean a *real* conversation. Not just 'how's it going today, Nathan?' Nothing like that. I'd like to come over to your house sometime and have a real conversation."

The girl shrugged and smiled, and Lucille saw the pulse beating in the girl's skinny neck, the faraway look in her eyes. Young girls could do that, Lucille remembered; they could take themselves away from what was happening to a place where it wasn't and wait there until it stopped. As Nathan stood there waiting for her answer, Lucille felt her own heart begin to beat faster. This was Nathan now, this was his life. It was all there, as if nothing had ever left him. The child who'd run to her, the angry kid who sat under the angry rain of his music, the fatherless boy with the beautiful shining hair, who frightened girls with his need and intensity.

The girl shrugged again. "We'll see, Nathan," she said, and just then a man put a pineapple onto the conveyor belt. The girl spun toward the customer, and her hair floated out behind her as she turned. Lucille watched Nathan watch it fly. She saw how much he wanted to touch it.

"Hi, how are you today?" the girl said brightly.

Nathan retreated to his bagging station at the end of the counter. He looked bewildered and groggy, as though he'd just waked up in an unfamiliar place. "Paper or plastic?" he asked.

"Plastic is good," the man said.

"Plastic it is, then," her son said, and he peeled a bag from the bunch that hung on the metal stand at the end of the counter. With a flourish, he snapped it open and reached for the pineapple and popped it into the bag with a tight smile. The man looked at him in a puzzled, irritated way. She did not want to see how this would end, so she stepped back and walked away, out through the produce, through the buckets of cut flowers and out the door. The ethereal voice stopped.

She was crossing the parking lot toward her car when she saw Nathan's familiar black Corolla with a line of new white lettering across the top of the windshield. What was he up to now? Closer, and she saw that the words were written upside down and backwards, like the secret code he used to write as a kid, sly notes slipped to her and Peter that could only be read in a mirror. *Dear Mom and Dad, By the time you figure out how to read this, I'll be a long way from here.* She'd saved that one, she didn't know why. Maybe because the effort and imagination he'd put into writing it had seemed promising.

It took her a minute to translate this latest message. *Slower Traffic Keep Right!* She edged around to the driver's side and rested her head against the car roof. It was hot, but she didn't care. She imagined how frightened a person might be, seeing those words appear in his rear view mirror. She lifted her head and looked around wildly. Where was Peter? She needed to talk to him right away. Why is Nathan's life such a mess? she wanted to ask him. What had she or he or *they* done to make their son so scary and forlorn and mistaken about almost everything? What does he want so desperately? she asked Peter.

What does anyone want? he said, in his calm, matter-of-fact way. To be seen through the dark glass of our troubles, to be loved for—or in spite of—ourselves.

In the dressing room at the Y, she stripped off her clothes and stepped into her old, faded, red bathing suit. She smoothed the suit down over her hips and faced herself in the full-length mirror beside the sink. A fifty-year-old woman looked back. Thin and a little stringy, a little gaunt. Muscle and sinew strung tight over bone. It was always a surprise to look in the mirror and meet the woman you were, not the one you wanted to be.

Three months earlier, her period had stopped. Now that was simplicity for you. The body cutting its ties, releasing its claim on the future. She turned the whirlpool jets on high and watched as the water began to roll. She walked down the steps and into the bubbling pool and stood with her back to the strongest jet. She felt the water shove and pummel her, but she planted her feet and stood firm. She thought of how Jesus had sent people down into the water to be healed. This was a parable, of course, like the loaves and fishes, a story of simple and miraculous transformation, the idea that you could go into the water broken and come up whole, that there would always be enough food and that the lives of those you loved moved toward goodness, but people trusted those stories as if they were promises.

They—and she, yes, she was one of them—ate their bread and washed themselves and wanted more of what they had and also what they didn't have. Even if they wanted less, they wanted *more* less. It was that simple.

Hush

When Jeffrey insisted on going to Mammoth Cave one month after the doctor at Sloan-Kettering stopped chemo, his wife Maureen called him her Uri Geller. Of course, she said, the difference between a Russian illusionist who bent a fork with his mind and her very sick husband was that Jeffrey was bending his *life*. What she meant was that the cancer found in one lung five years ago had spread to his spine and brain, and he still hadn't given up. Whenever one doctor ran out of options, they found another. They'd flown all over the country and even to Mexico, tracking down doctors who would cut out more lung tissue or seed the tumors with radioactive isotopes. *My miracle man,* Maureen called him, their mantra, every time another procedure briefly distracted the cancer.

"I have my reasons," he said when Maureen asked why he wanted to go to Mammoth Cave, but reasons were not all he had. One month earlier, after the oncologist's verdict, he'd sent Maureen back to the hotel to lie down, then picked up the book she'd brought him, a guide to the National Parks illustrated with majestic color photographs. He closed his eyes and whispered, "Now where?" and he let the book fall open across his bony legs. When he opened his eyes again, he was looking into a vaulted chamber in Mammoth Cave, Kentucky, and he asked himself why he'd been shown that picture so soon after he'd been told to make peace with what he hadn't done and would never have or be, if he wasn't meant to go there?

"Really, Jeffrey?" he imagined Maureen saying. "The book fell open and you think that's a sign?" She was no believer in signs and portents, and neither was he, before he got sick, so he told her he'd always wanted to see the cave, and she didn't ask again. He didn't want to frighten her the way he frightened himself when he considered the distance that lay between the rational healthy man he'd been and the superstitious sick man he'd turned into, who watched for signs the way a person might search the night sky for a glimpse of the satellite of hope. In the last six months, the healthy man had been dwindling faster and faster, like a man seen in the rear view mirror of a speeding car, or through the wrong end of a telescope. Now the gap between them was so wide, the sick man hardly remembered the healthy man.

So he and his sturdy, loyal wife left their kids, Emily and Matthew, with his brother for the weekend and went down to Kentucky. Now they waited outside an entrance into Mammoth Cave for the ranger to arrive and start the tour. By Maureen's watch it was 2:06; the tour was supposed to start at 2. At 2:08, the ranger ambled down the path toward their group like he was in no hurry to get anywhere. He was a young guy with a broad, merry face, a neat ginger-colored mustache and cold blue eyes.

At the educational software company Jeffrey founded—and had run so brilliantly that classrooms all over the country used its products—no one was late for anything more than once. The healthy man he'd been reached to brush back a crisp shirt cuff and show the ranger his watch. Then he saw the hands that gripped the handle of his aluminum cane and remembered why he'd stopped wearing a watch.

When the ranger walked to the front of the tour group and said, "Welcome, folks, everybody ready?" Maureen held Jeffrey close, the way she did before he went into an operating room, her cheek pressed hard against his breastbone. When he'd told her he wanted to take this tour alone, she hadn't argued; they almost never argued now, about anything. I'll be fine, he told her, and he believed it. He'd gained a few pounds since leaving the hospital. He had his cane and a water bottle clipped to his belt; he had the nerve and guts and discipline that had gotten him this far. *A coward dies a thousand deaths,* his father used to say. *A brave man only one.* A soldier's paraphrase of Shakespeare that the old man had picked up in the Pacific and lived by for the rest of his life.

Jeffrey smoothed Maureen's hair, felt her breathe against him. In the sun, her auburn hair looked rich and fiery, but in the last five years, gray had inched out from the crown as though ashes had been dumped on her head.

There were ten of them in the tour group, and as they started down the narrow, hard-packed dirt trail, Jeffrey claimed first place in line behind the ranger. Cancer or no cancer, the drive to be first hadn't left him. At home, he rousted his kids out of bed the way his father had rousted him. *Ripper-dipper and lots of pepper. Give yourself a lecture.* In college, he'd been captain of the

93

fencing team, and during one legendary tournament, he'd driven his opponent down the floor and up against the back wall of the gym with such ferocity the other boy could only parry and retreat; he never once took the offensive. The photograph of Jeffrey taken after he'd led the team to the NCAA championship still hung in the coach's office, and he'd heard that the team lined up before an important competition to touch the tip of their foils to his sweaty, victorious face, for good luck.

After the first round of surgery and chemo, he'd joined a group of other people with grim diagnoses—survivors they were encouraged to call themselves. Following the psychologist's instructions, they closed their eyes and conjured an image of some powerful, personal force doing battle with their disease. He'd pictured himself in fencing gear, driving the cancer back, his foil flashing like lightning.

Around the first bend in the trail, the daylight disappeared. High up on the cave walls, a string of bare, dim bulbs glowed like a memory of light. As they walked, the ranger recited cave history and facts. His voice, echoing off the walls, sounded oracular. The cave temperature was a constant fifty-four degrees, he said. The slave Stephen Bishop was the first to cross The Bottomless Pit. In the nineteenth century a Dr. Croghan had built a tuberculosis sanitarium in one of the cave's deep chambers, believing that if he could remove his patients from the reach of the solar influences, they might be healed. "Was he right?" Jeffrey asked the man's broad back.

The ranger stopped, turned hitched up his belt. As most people did now, the ranger glanced at his face and looked away. He didn't blame the man. These days he couldn't look himself in the eye for long either, because of what looked back at him. "Well, sir," the ranger said. "It seems the good doctor forget to account for the smoke from cooking fires and torches. "Bottom line," he said. "They all died." A whiff of the military hovered around him, like aftershave. Jeffrey saw his own father's grim hilarity in the ranger's eyes. *The joke's on you,* seemed to be the lesson that most of his father's war stories taught, and for much of his life, Jeffrey had lived as though he got it.

The ranger turned and walked on, pointing out pictographs and smudges of ash where ancient Indians had daubed their torches, leaving marks to guide them through the cave's labyrinth. The tour group followed, moving down between the sheer walls and piles of slate rubble, and Jeffrey kept his place at the head of the line and waited for fatigue to overwhelm him, and when it didn't, he took that as a sign, and he smiled. "I'm only forty-five," he reminded himself. Another mantra. Down, down, down they moved until the path widened and they walked into the tall chamber he'd seen in the book the day he'd asked for a sign. They were standing under a high stone ceiling that rippled like water. A slow-moving river ran along the base of the rear wall, and in this river, according to the guidebook, eyeless fish had evolved to swim the lightless depths. Sometimes it took a while, Jeffrey thought, but nature always managed to eliminate the superfluous.

In the middle of the chamber, the ranger stopped. "Gather round, folks," he said, and he switched off his enormous, black flashlight and moved to a breaker box on the wall. The crown of his hat sent a long shadow up the chamber's rear wall. "We are presently one hundred feet underground. When I extinguish these lights," he said, "you will experience pure night." Pure night. The ranger savored the words as if he liked their taste, and Jeffrey wondered whether the man had come up with the phrase himself or someone else had written it for him. So much was scripted these days. Stewardesses, nurses, customer service representatives, all asking how your day was going, assuring you they understood how you felt. All echoes and phantoms of feeling that left you longing for the real thing.

While a young couple fumbled at their flashlights, the ranger smiled patiently, evidently used to waiting for people to give up their little lights and follow him into the dark. Then he pulled the handle on the breaker box and the sickly lights on the walls flared once and went out. A man said, "Boo," and a few people laughed. Then they all got quiet.

A palpable darkness descended as though the stone of the roof and walls had breathed it out. It dropped and settled, soft and heavy, over their group, and though Jeffrey's eyes were open, he saw nothing. Pure night was the right way to describe this darkness; there was no give to it, no crack or fault that light might find. Nothing within or beyond it but itself. A darkness that flooded every channel of sight. He held out his hands, saw nothing of himself, and when he touched his face, he startled, as though a stranger had touched him. He was grateful for the breathing of his fellow tourists.

He closed his eyes and moved deeper into the darkness until there seemed no place where he stopped and the darkness began. He remembered the doctor's answer when Jeffrey asked him what happened when your time came. "That's an excellent question," the doctor said. At Sloan-Kettering he'd been endlessly complimented on his questions. A script they learned in medical school, no doubt, another echo.

"Where is the cancer likely to go next?"

"Good question."

"What's our next move?"

"An excellent question."

At his last session with the oncologist, just after the verdict came down, Jeffrey pushed a notepad across his bed tray. "Write it down for me," he said, but the doctor pushed the notepad back. "Come on, man," Jeffrey said. "It's not a contract. What you say will not be used against you."

"When the lower organs start to fail," the doctor said, looking down at his hands, "the heart tries to pump blood to the site of the failure. When the heart begins to falter, the lungs send more oxygen to the heart. The body finally loses, but it never gives up," he said. Then he looked at Jeffrey and said it again—"it never gives up"—as though it might be comforting to hear those words repeated.

"Thank you," Jeffrey said, and he meant it.

Now he leaned on his cane and tried to remember the last time Maureen had believed in him. The day he was released from Sloan-Kettering, she sat beside his bed and held his hand, moving her thumb over the peaks and valleys of his knuckles. "You're my miracle man, Jeffrey," she said, level-eyed as ever, but the familiar words had sounded frayed and unconvincing. He wondered if she was ready for him to give up and do what he was told. Not that he blamed her; he didn't blame anyone anymore for wanting what they wanted. Down in this pure night, he was starting to feel how it might be to let go, become a smudge of ash on the wall of the cave of the world, and he wondered if this were the sign he'd been brought here to see.

"So be it," he said to himself, and he felt the silence deepen around and within him. Take away the sound of breathing, he thought, and the silence would be as pure and complete as the night. If he were in charge, he'd ask everyone to hold their breath and let the earth's deep silence flow into the darkness, until it formed a great river that swept all the eyeless fish away. Then he heard whispering. At first it was as faint as the whisking of two pieces of paper brushed together, then it got louder, and he turned, anger surging his chest. No doubt, the whisperer belonged to that tribe who balked at rules and limitations, the ones who drove through stop signs they found inconvenient, yakked on their cell phones anywhere. The tribe where he'd once been king.

"Hush," he hissed.

"Oh, *please,*" a woman hissed back. "Who do you think you are?"

The question frightened him, as though the darkness itself had asked it. *Who do I think I am?*

An eyeless fish. Eldest son. Husband to Maureen, father to Emily and Matthew. Names from a eulogy, all of them. Names from a finished life. What answer would a living man give? A man who wanted to live?

"I don't know," he whispered, and then he said it again, because the words sounded good in the dark. "I don't know." It was a relief to feel so hesitant, so uncertain, and the hard wedge of dread in his chest softened. Surely the forces of goodness and mercy that were said to follow us through all our days would not let him die with that question unanswered. Head bowed, he listened and waited to be asked again.

Soon

Elizabeth Long Crawford was born with a lazy eye, and so, one morning when she was twelve, her father and the doctor sat her down in the dining room at Marlcrest, the Long family place near Augusta, Georgia, and told her they were going to fix her so a man would want to marry her someday. Her father held her on his lap while the doctor pressed a handkerchief soaked with chloroform over her nose and mouth, and she went under, dreaming of the beauty she would be. But the doctor's hand slipped, and when Elizabeth woke up, she was blind in her right eye. What she remembered of that morning, she told her children, were the last sights she'd seen through two good eyes: the shadows of leaves on the sunny floor, the hair on the backs of her father's hands, the stripe on the doctor's trousers, the handkerchief coming down. Then blindness. The rise and the downfall of hope, one complete revolution of the wheel that turned the world, that's what she'd lived through.

Marlcrest was a hard name to pronounce. The first syllable sprawled, it wouldn't be hurried; the second climbed a height and looked down on the rest of the world, and so did Elizabeth. It had been a hard place to live, too. One hundred acres of level, sandy land on a bluff above the Savannah River, and a house raised high on brick pillars to offer the people of the house a view of the river, a chance at the river breezes. When Elizabeth married Perry Crawford, he'd agreed to live there, too. *She* wasn't leaving. In the family cemetery on the bluff stood the Long tomb and the graves of the children who'd died at birth, who had fallen or been trampled by horses or killed by cholera or yellow fever during the two hundred years the Longs had lived at Marlcrest.

Before the Civil War, slaves hauled muck up from the river—the *marl* of which the *crest* was made—to spread on the fields. Many died there: smothered in mud, collapsed in the heat, snake-bit, drowned. They were buried in a corner of a distant field that the pine woods had taken back years before Elizabeth's daughter Martha was born, though even in Martha's time a wandering child could still find broken crockery, shells, empty brown medicine bottles under the pine needles, as if the people buried there had been given back to the earth by others who trusted that the dead could be comforted and fed.

After the botched operation, Martha's mother lived where the wheel had stopped and she'd stepped off. The blind eye that the doctor had closed gave her a proud, divided look, as though half her face slept while the other stayed fiercely alert, on the lookout for the next violation or betrayal. She'd looked that way—disfigured and ferocious—just after her seventy-fifth birthday when she summoned Martha and her brother, Perry Jr., to the nursing home in Augusta to hear some exciting news. They'd put her there after a series of small strokes had made it dangerous for her to live alone at Marlcrest.

For six months before they moved her to the home, there had been crisis after crisis. She stopped payment on every check. The doors of the house, inside and out, filled up with locks. Her nightly phone calls to her children were packed with complaint. The woman they hired to stay with her was a tippler. Someone was downstairs, picking the locks. It was that Herbert Long from up the road. He or one of his family, descendants of the slaves who'd once lived on the place. For a hundred years they'd bided their time; now they'd come to rob her.

At the nursing home that day, their mother sat in her wheelchair in front of the sunny window. She was dressed in beige linen, her best earrings, her heirloom pearls. Her hair had been freshly restored to a cresting silver wave, and she smelled of Arpège perfume, the scent of all her finest hours.

"Well, don't you look nice, Mother. What's the occasion?" Martha asked, kissing her mother's sweet, powdered cheek.

Some papers in their mother's purse, that was the occasion. Smiling brilliantly, she handed over the documents. She'd sold Marlcrest—the whole kit and caboodle—to a developer who would bulldoze the house, clear the land, build a subdivision there. Plantation Oaks, he'd call it. "Here is a copy of the title deed," she said, passing it to Perry Jr. "As you will see, it is properly executed." He turned it over, held it up to the light looking for errors, finding none.

As for the family records and belongings—the *contents* of the house, she said, leaning toward them from her wheelchair with her hands folded in her lap and high color in her cheeks, savoring (Martha saw) the vengeful triumph of this theft—she'd sold them all to a young man from a southern history museum in Atlanta. She struck the wheelchair's armrest. *Done.* He'd been coming to visit her in this terrible place since her children had put her there—it had been almost exactly one year now. He'd even driven her out to Marlcrest a few times in his own automobile to pick up something she'd been forbidden to bring with her. The Long family had many possessions of historical interest; already the museum people were calling their belongings the most important collection of southern artifacts ever acquired in Georgia. Fine cotton lawn shirts and baby gowns sewed by slave seamstresses. Diaries and ledgers and sharecropper contracts. Tools, portraits. A complete record of plantation life. The young man had been so sweet to her. He had all the time in the world to sit and talk. He never sneaked looks at his watch or found some excuse to jump up and rush off five minutes after he sat down.

Not that Martha and Perry Jr. hadn't been expecting it somehow. They'd lived their lives braced for such blows. The hurt that's been lived will be handed on. Their mother always said she lived by *high ideals,* which meant that everything had to be right, but since nothing ever was right, she was constantly, deeply, and bitterly disappointed by every person and every circumstance.

Horsey had been her word for Martha, and it summed up her daughter's flaws and lacks. A long face, big teeth, lank hair, eyes that shone with dark, equine clarity. Martha was also too *big,* too fleshy. She sweated in the summer heat, and in the winter her fingertips stayed cold. Perry Jr. was never more than an adequate student, a lukewarm son. Even her husband, Perry Sr., failed her. When Martha was sixteen and Perry Jr. had just turned eighteen, their father sneaked off early one October morning to shoot ducks in the swamp below the old slave burying ground, and there he had a fatal heart attack. After dark the sheriff found him in the duck blind, still seated on his camp stool with his gun across his knees, his head resting against the small window hole in the wall, as though he were watching the mallards flash and preen in the dark water below.

His death enraged their mother, and afterwards she widened her search for the thief who'd robbed her. And yet, though Martha and Perry Jr. had both expected that someday their mother would get to their names on her long list of suspects in the crimes against her, neither was prepared for it. Is anyone *prepared* for the actuality of life, which is always more surprising or horrifying or sweet than we could ever have imagined? Not at all. We dream and wish and plan, but something more subtle, more generous, more devious, arranges reality for us.

After their mother finished telling them how she'd sold their birthright, she leaned back, satisfied, and looked at her children with that brilliant and terrible *any questions?* look on her face.

Martha closed her eyes. She saw the bulldozer push the house. It swayed, cracked, fell, carrying beds, tables, chairs, her grandmother's round hat boxes and furs, the river's wide curve that she could see from her bedroom window in winter when the leaves had fallen and the trees along the river banks were bare. Carrying the slave cemetery, where just that past spring Martha had found plastic lilies in a Mason jar on a weeded grave. That day in the nursing home, for the first time, Martha felt the world fail and move away from her the way her mother had promised it would, not with words exactly—though Elizabeth had certainly given her children enough of those—but with her footsteps walking away from them, her closed face, her fury.

Their mother died less than a year from that day. Just after dinner on a rainy Saturday evening in early June, she had a stroke of a magnitude that even *she* might have judged to be a fitting cause of death for a person of her stature and standing, a force so powerful it knocked her out of her wheelchair and left her dead on the floor before the first hand touched her.

At the viewing Martha was startled to see her mother looking different in an unexpected way. The perfect wave of silver hair was intact, as were the long, elegant fingers, and yet, without the ferocious hauteur it wore in life, her face looked wasted, starved, as if under the rage a ravenous sadness had been at work. Not even the undertaker's crafted composure, the small rueful smile he'd shaped on her mouth, or the kindly light from the pink light bulbs in the sconces on the funeral home walls could soften the face she would wear now into eternity.

2.

What do you do with what you've been given? Martha would not have her children murmuring *poor Mother* over her coffin. She went back to the life she'd made for herself, a calm, ordinary life, firmly planted life. As Martha saw it, her mother's bitterness and rage were exactly as large and violent as her hopes and longings, and so it was these longings that Martha would uproot in herself.

That's why she'd married Raymond Maitland (against her mother's wishes), a decent man from a decent family of textile mill people, a big, careful, sober man with jug ears who wanted what she wanted.

They lived in the country outside of Augusta, and Raymond, a salesman, traveled up and down the coast, only he called it the *eastern seaboard,* because he believed the high-minded sound of those words gave him a competitive edge over his coarser peers. His territory stretched from Myrtle Beach, South Carolina, to Jacksonville, Florida, and at one time or another, he sold insurance, vending machine snacks, and office supplies. For years, the drawers in their kitchen and den filled up with pencils, ballpoint pens, rulers, rubber jar-lid openers, key chains, thermometers, and spatulas, all printed with the names and slogans of companies he represented.

In the spring, summer, and early fall, he drove with the windows rolled down (this was in the fifties, before cars were air conditioned), his left arm resting on the window ledge, so that his arm was always sunburned after a sales trip. At home, it was one of their pleasures for him to shower, lie on their bed in his undershorts with the fan blowing across him and the radio tuned to the light classics station, while she rubbed Solarcaine on his sunburned arm as gently and patiently as if his skin were her skin, so that he imagined sometimes that the spreading cool relief came directly from her fingertips, their delicate, swirling touch.

Then one day in late July, the summer Raymond, Sr. was fifty-eight and Martha had just turned fifty-six, the summer Raymond Jr. finished graduate school at Georgia Tech and their daughter Louise had her second baby, Raymond returned from a week-long trip to South Carolina. He traveled for Tom's Peanut Company then. He threw his car keys onto the kitchen counter and fell into her arms, groaning about the six hundred miles he had just driven through the *goddamn* heat, and at his age, too. He smelled of fry grease and cigarette smoke subtly overlaid with sweat and metal, the smell of the road. Someday, he said, they'd find him slumped over the steering wheel on the shoulder of some sweltering back road through the Pee Dee swamp. A desk job, that's what he wanted now. To keep him closer to home, closer to *her,* that was the ticket.

"Take a shower," she said. "Come lie down."

While she rubbed the cream into his arm, she felt the silky slackness of aging flesh under her hands; she saw that his muscles were starting to droop, go ropy. His chest had begun to sag, too. And as she tenderly catalogued the marks of time on her husband's body, she noticed that his left arm was as pale as the rest of him. She looked at the small, pleased, and peaceful smile on his mouth. She sat on the edge of the bed in the breeze from the fan, the Solarcaine squeezed onto her fingers, and a picture rose up to meet her as though his body had released it: a woman in green shorts lounging in a white wicker chair, her big tanned legs crossed, smoking a cigarette and laughing.

She rubbed the Solarcaine into his pale arm. Next day she went through the phone bills for the last six months, found call after call to a number in Little River, South Carolina. The voice that answered when Martha called the number matched the thick legs, the cigarettes, the indolence of the woman whose image had wormed its way into her mind. That night, when she showed him the phone bills, Raymond put his hands over his face and cried. It was true, he'd gotten in over his head. He would break off with—"Don't you dare speak her name in my house," Martha shrieked—if Martha would just be patient and give him time. If she would just forgive him.

Patience she had, and time. Plenty of both, and the will to forgive, too. For six months they tried, but it had gone too far with the other woman. The story came out one shard at a time: the jewelry he'd given her, a semester's tuition for her son at the University of South Carolina, the promises he'd made. She was a widow, twenty years younger than Martha. It almost drove Martha crazy. Just when she thought she'd heard the whole story, he'd choke out another piece until it seemed there was no end to the future he'd planned with this woman.

When Raymond left to go live in Little River with his big-legged woman, Martha told him she wanted two things—no, make that three, she wanted three things: she wanted the house in Augusta, and the house in Scaly Mountain. Louise and Raymond Jr. had been in grade school when Raymond and Martha had bought a beat-up old white clapboard house two stories tall and one room wide, roofed with tin, that sat on a foundation of stacked stones in a valley at the foot of Scaly Mountain, North Carolina; they went there every summer and at Thanksgiving, too, if they could manage it. When they got there, Raymond had to be first out of the car. "Let Daddy have his minute," she'd say to the children. He'd make a big show of stretching and breathing, as if he couldn't get enough of that air. Then he'd stand with his hands on his hips, his chest thrown out, king of the hill. Next he'd lean his elbows on the car door, push his wide smiling face through the open window, squeeze her arm and say, "We're fifty-cent millionaires, Martha, sure enough." Meaning it didn't take much to make him feel wealthy. Meaning what he had was everything he wanted. Then he'd kiss her richly on the mouth, and they had arrived.

The third thing she wanted from Raymond was never to hear from him again. She meant it, too, about cutting him out of her life for good. She knew the way to the cold, bare space inside herself where she could live by the absolutes she declared. Goodbye, Raymond. "I thank my mother for the strength she instilled in me," she told Louise during the divorce. "No, really. She's the one who gave me the backbone for this." Finishing cleanly, she meant, cutting the cord.

3.

Five years after the divorce, Martha announced that she was moving to the house in Scaly Mountain. "My thermostat must be broken, I can't take this heat any longer," she told Louise, who was frantic about her mother's moving so far away, and all alone, too. "What if you fall?" Louise asked. "What if you have a stroke or a heart attack?"

"Friend, come up higher," Martha joked with her friends from the Episcopal church when they asked her if she'd thought through what she was doing. She told others that she was retiring. From what? they demanded to know. From what? From canasta on Monday and bridge on Tuesday (she did not say), from standing in the vestibule before Sunday morning services, alert for a new face. ("Welcome to All Saints. Are you visiting with us this morning? Would you please fill out this card and drop it in the collection basket?") From taping books for the blind and pushing the book cart through the hospital corridors, intruding on the desperately ill, challenging them with her smile to buck up. From muffins and casseroles and sympathy calls and notes of congratulation or consolation. From rushing to church every time the doors swung open or having to explain her absence to some anxious friend. Goodbye to all that.

She did not tell anyone about the solitude she craved: to be alone, with new vistas in front of her eyes and unfamiliar, rocky ground below her feet. Nor did she speak of how she longed to be rid of Raymond. The house—her house—still smelled of his cigarette smoke. The week before she decided to move, she'd come across a crushed package of Tom's cheese crackers in the back of a kitchen drawer, and at that moment she'd known that this house would always be pushing up reminders of Raymond, no matter how hard she scrubbed and bleached and aired.

He rested more lightly on the mountain house. There, she could lift a few T-shirts out of the bottom drawer of the bedroom dresser and tear them into rags; she could break his coffee mug, rip his handwritten instructions off the wall between the hot-water heater and furnace. Then he would be gone for good, the way her mother was gone. The mother whose grave she visited dutifully twice a year, carrying a poinsettia at Christmas, a lily at Eastertime, where she stood with her head bowed, her heart empty of any longing to see her mother, or speak to her or hear her voice.

But a living, breathing person can't just do *nothing*, can she? Can't sit all day with her hands folded or a game of solitaire spread out on the kitchen table. Can't stop talking to other people without hearing crazy echoes coming back from the solo conversation with herself. So, once she'd settled into the Scaly Mountain house, she went to work. She had the pasture behind the house mowed and dammed the creek to make a pond. She added two rooms and a porch to the back of the house, and she lengthened the kitchen until the house looked like a white, wooden shirt with outstretched arms. Twice a week, she drove her white Dodge Dart over the mountain to the senior center in Highlands, for canasta and talk.

Every week she wrote long letters full of questions and advice to her children. "Have Sarah Lynn's teeth shown any signs of straightening?" she wrote to Louise. "If not, do *please* take her to the orthodontist." "Those old linen napkins I gave you are to be used as *tea towels*," she wrote after she'd visited Louise and found the napkins balled up in the rag basket under the kitchen sink. Her daughter's letters were long and chatty, with fabric swatches stapled to them or pictures of the children enclosed. Raymond Jr. wrote his full-speed-ahead notes on "Memo from Raymond Maitland, Jr." paper. He was a big executive at Coca-Cola down in Atlanta, she told her friends over the canasta table. Very big, she'd repeat, arching her eyebrows to show that words simply could not measure the heights he'd climbed.

Every week, without fail, she wrote to her brother. After his wife died, he'd drifted into mysticism, joined the Rosicrucians. His letters were about the migration of souls, the power of the spirit to transcend time and space, to enter that place where there was no death, no beginning or end, only a current that carried you endlessly higher toward the realm of fulfillment and bliss. Someday he would join his wife in that kingdom, he wrote. He could hardly wait for that day.

Martha sat at the desk in her bedroom in the house she'd claimed and made her own—a plain, tall woman in a sleeveless blouse and a full skirt made of a coarse, rustic material like burlap. Her braids were crossed and pinned over the top of her head; she wore orthopedic sandals with wool socks and she sat in a high-backed chair with her ankles crossed, her back very straight.

One must be *realistic,* she wrote to her brother, apply the styptic pencil to one's scratches, pour iodine into the deeper wounds, get on with life in *this* world. Reality (she underlined it twice) was a constant and trustworthy companion that, once befriended, never let one down or walked away and loved someone else. A person must not wear himself out with wanting what was impossible to have. What was finished must be done with and put away.

"False hopes are cruel, Perry," she wrote. "We must not exhaust ourselves with longing for what will never be. I speak from experience when I say this. As you well know, I have suffered indignities at the hands of life—haven't we all—but the longer I live the more certain I become that the consolations of life—if any—must be sought and found in facing life squarely, as it is. The mind must not be allowed to wander where it wants, else it might end up lost in a wilderness of longing and regret. This I believe."

She'd lived in Scaly Mountain for a year. The pond was full, the meadow fenced, the hay rolled and drying in the field she'd leased to a neighbor. One September evening she sat on the porch after supper, watching the last light flood the valley and spread across the foot of her meadow, gilding the fat rolls of hay. The Long family Bible lay open on her lap to the page where she'd just written her mother's name and the date of her death.

This was no modest Sunday school Bible with a white pebbled cover and a tiny gold cross dangling from a red-ribbon marker. It was the original family Bible in which family births, weddings, and deaths had been recorded since 1825. A serious and heavy book with a tooled leather cover, a lock and key. It smelled of the smoke of many fires, and its registry pages were stained and soft as cloth. When her father had opened it for family devotions, Martha used to imagine thunder rolling off its pages.

After her mother sold everything, Martha went to Marlcrest and without hesitation, without guilt, she lifted the Bible from the carved wooden stand next to the fireplace in the downstairs parlor, where it had rested throughout her life and her mother's life and her mother's and her mother's, and she'd taken it home. For a year, the museum wrote to her about the Bible. They were tentative, respectful letters at first. Later, letters from lawyers began to arrive. She ignored them all.

Now, as she looked from her mother's name out to the meadow, she felt time catch and roll over, the way tumblers move inside a big lock. Maybe it was the way the golden light slanted across the fat rolls of hay that invited the sensation. Maybe it was the sight of the ink drying on the page or a confluence of all of those things, but she felt herself lifted, carried, and moved one place closer to the head of the line her mother had vacated.

That's when the idea of the reunion came to her. She would summon what was left of the Long clan to this place and celebrate their long history. The next morning she drove into Highlands and ordered stationery with *Long Family Reunion* embossed across the top. She set the date for the following summer: July 6–9, 1969. All winter she wrote letters and logged in the answers, then sent back diagrams of the house with rooms and beds assigned.

Give Martha time, her brother used to say, and she could plan anything. Perry Jr. had landed in France on D-Day; he always said that Martha could have planned the Normandy invasion better than Ike had done. She'd certainly planned *this*. She'd drawn twenty-five far-flung Longs to her place, then stood in the parking lot she'd made in her meadow and waved them to their designated spaces with a flashlight, like a state trooper at a football game. She carried their suitcases and marched them up to the house and directed them to their rooms.

For the children there were relay races and treasure hunts and nature hikes down the valley with Martha at the head of the column, like the Scout leader she'd been when Louise was growing up, a walking encyclopedia of the ways of trees, reptiles, birds and stones. For the grownups there was plenty of food and talk; the family Bible and old, cracked photographs passed from hand to hand. All week, a scroll as big as a blueprint, the Long family tree, hung on the dining room wall.

At night there were games and prizes. A prize for the oldest Long, a dim old uncle, ninety-three that summer, who sat patiently wherever he was put until someone moved him. And for the youngest, a son born in the spring to Lamar Long and his wife June, just after Lamar had been promoted to foreman of the weave room at the Bibb Mill in Porterdale, Georgia. A blue baby, they called him, born with a defective valve in his heart. A good baby, all eyes, who lay quietly in his basket studying the faces that drifted like clouds across his sky.

Wasn't Martha the bossiest woman in the world? they whispered among themselves. Exactly like her mother, the older ones said. Poor soul. Even her own brother had to butt heads with her. One morning he came whistling into the kitchen, intending to skim a dollop of cream for his coffee from one of the bottles of raw milk that Martha was so adamant about making them all drink. So much healthier than pasteurized milk, she said. Right behind Perry came Martha, and she plucked the bottle out of his hand before he'd shut the refrigerator door. "Perry," she said. "I'm saving this to go on top of the blackberry pie I shall make for the farewell dinner. You can't have any."

"Oh, come on, Martha, I only want a teaspoon," he said.

"I cannot spare that much," she said, and for half an hour they went back and forth like that.

Finally, Perry broke. "I want some of that damn cream, Martha," he said holding out his cup. "Just a smidgen for my coffee."

"Well, you can't have it, Perry," she said. "I told you. I need all of it for the pie. She held the bottle out to show him—not the yellow clot in the neck of the bottle, but the cream, the *cream,* whipped into high, stiff points and the warm, rich pie beneath that sweet, smothering layer. Couldn't he see it? She could, and the thought of that cream-to-be made tears stand in her eyes. Then the fact that she was crying over *whipped cream* made her furious. She who'd written to her brother about dignity and the pitfalls of looking too far into the future or the past for happiness or consolation, she who'd thrown the force of her considerable will into living in the world as it *is.*

Finally Perry Jr. slammed his coffee cup on the kitchen counter and walked out. "I had to lock horns with Martha today," he said that night to Lamar Long, and a child who overhead that remark and the laughter that followed pictured two warring moose in a mountain meadow, their enormous antlers locked, shoving each other until they collapsed and died. Then the passing seasons, then the bones, the bleached antlers still entangled.

On the last day of the reunion, according to plan, Martha climbed the rickety wooden stepladder and strung Japanese paper lanterns between the big silver maple beside the road and the cedar nearest the house. At six-fifteen they would eat, followed at seven by speeches, testimonials, recollections, a song or two, and a final word from the family genealogist, who'd traced the clan back to England. Tonight, he would name for them the place from which the first Longs had embarked for the New World. Exactly at six, Martha struck a small silver bell with a silver fork and waited until its clear note had died away, then invited everyone to line up, oldest to youngest, as she'd planned. They filed past the tables made of sawhorses and planks and covered with white cloths and filled their plates. Chicken and corn and beans—they heaped it on—banana pudding and coconut cake and, of course, Martha's blackberry pie topped with a mountain range of whipped cream.

They'd just settled down to supper when she heard Abel Rankin's wagon coming down the road. He was her neighbor, the one who sold her the raw milk out of cans that he carried in the back of his wagon, that wholesome milk from which she'd saved *all* the cream. She heard the clink of the cans, the wagon's jolting rattle, the jingle of the bridle on Sawdust the mule and the stumbling crack of his hooves on the rocky road. She filled a plate with chicken, beans and coconut cake and walked out to the edge of the road to wait for him. When Abel Rankin saw her, he reined Sawdust in and said, "Evening" (never quite meeting her eyes), touched the brim of his brown felt hat, and took the plate of food she held up to him. "Eat this, Mr. Rankin," she said.

He ate quickly, hunched over on the wagon seat as though eating were a chore he had to finish before dark, while she held Sawdust's bridle, patted his face, felt the bony plank of his nose, his breath on her hands. When the children came running to pat the mule, she took charge. She made them line up and listen to her. "Now, stroke his nose lightly," she said. "You stroke an animal as lightly as you'd stroke a hummingbird. You want him to remember you?" she asked. "Blow into his nostrils. Gently, *gently*, you hear me talking to you?"

Those were her mother's teachings, her mother's actual *words*. As soon as they'd left her mouth, she felt her mother walk up behind her and stand there, listening to hear if what she'd said about the treatment of mules was right. Her mother had kept a reservoir of tenderness toward animals unpolluted by her general disappointment and bitterness. No animal had ever betrayed her. Oh, no. When Martha was a child, there had always been a pack of half-starved stray dogs skulking around the back steps at Marlcrest, waiting for her mother's charity. There had always been a shoebox on top of the stove full of baby squirrels rescued from a fallen pine, tenderly wrapped in flannel and bottle-fed into independence.

Her mother had owned a Tennessee walking horse, a flashy bay named Jimbo, whose black mane and tail she'd braided with red ribbons before she rode him in shows. She used to nuzzle, stroke, pat the horse, bury her face in his mane, while Martha hung on the paddock fence, listening to the rich, dark warmth that filled her mother's voice when she talked to the horse, waiting for that warm and liquid love to overflow the dam in her mother's heart and pour onto her.

Waiting, still waiting. And now her mother stood so close that Martha imagined she heard her mother's breath whistling down the bony narrows of her imperial nose. Her mother, who'd traveled such a long way to find Martha and withhold her love again, just to remind her daughter, as a good mother should, that her love might still be won if Martha would be patient and not lose heart, if she would just get things right for a change.

Martha held her breath, then shook her head to clear it and turned to see if anyone had noticed her standing there like a fool with her eyes squeezed shut and an eager, hopeful look on her face. Up on the wagon seat, Abel Rankin worked steadily at his supper; the children cooed and stroked Sawdust's nose and laid their cheeks against his whiskery muzzle. Back in the yard, her people sat on the grass and on the porch, enjoying their food. They circled the table and filled their plates a second time, a third; they lifted thick slabs from her beautiful pie.

What a ridiculous old woman you are, she thought. Standing there waiting for your dead mother to love you. But there it was again, percolating up through the layers of years, this sly and relentless force that moved through the world, this patient and brutal need that people called hope, which would not be stopped, ever, in its work of knitting and piecing and binding, recovering, reclaiming, making whole. Which formed from the stuff of your present life a future where you would be healed or loved and sent you running forward while it dissolved and remade itself ahead of you, so that you lived always with the feeling, so necessary to survival in this world, that you were not just trudging along but moving *toward* something.

She guessed that if you could just give up hope, your time on earth would be free of longing and its disfigurements. God knows she'd tried. But you couldn't. Not even her mother had done that, finally. Even after she'd sold Marlcrest out from under them and momentarily righted the wrong of her life by taking from someone else what she felt had been taken from her, she hadn't been satisfied. Instead, she'd begun to pine and grieve for her old poodle.

Rowdy was his name. Martha's only inheritance. She'd taken him to her house when she and Perry Jr. put their mother in the home. He was thirteen years old then, morose and incontinent, a trembler, a fear-biter. Nothing left of him but gluey old eyes, a curly coat, and bones. One Saturday morning soon after he came to live with her, she left him for an hour while she went to the grocery store, and he turned over the garbage and ate a small Crisco can of bacon drippings. She found him on her kitchen floor, greasy and struggling to breathe, and rushed him to the vet's office where he died two hours later, his blood so clogged with fat his old heart just choked on it.

Until her dying day their mother had been greedy for news of Rowdy, and Martha and Perry Jr. had given it to her. They'd even pretended to be passing Rowdy back and forth between them, sharing the wealth. On one visit, Perry Jr. would tell their mother how Rowdy still had enough spark to chase squirrels around Perry's back yard on a cool fall morning. On the next visit, Martha would add to the story. Rowdy still enjoyed his dog biscuits, she'd say, even though he gummed them and it took him forever to eat one. He's a little constipated, she would say, but he's fine. "Well, then, you're not feeding him enough roughage," their mother would say. "Feed him apples. I must have told you that a thousand times, don't you listen when I talk to you?" she would say, the old meanness sharpening her good eye.

Then she would smile. Toward the end, when she smiled at them, it was her skull that smiled; then the weeping would begin. "Why don't you bring my little dog to see me?" she would sob. "Soon, Mother," they would promise, patting her hand, smoothing back her hair. "Next time."

4.

Now it's August, twenty-five years past the summer of the reunion. Olivia Hudson, one of Martha's grandnieces, is driving through the mountains with her husband and small son when they pass a road that runs up a narrow valley. "Remember my telling you about the family reunion?" she says. "That looks like the road to my great-aunt Martha's house." She'd been seven that summer, the blue baby was her brother; in one photograph she leans over his basket, smiling, while he holds tight to her finger. Now they turn back and head up the valley, and as they drive Olivia studies the landscape. She cannot imagine that the house is still standing, but she hopes that some arrangement of trees and pastures and fences will rebuild it in her mind's eye and set it down on its lost foundation. She hopes for sheets of roofing tin, a standing chimney, steps leading up to an overgrown field. Any trace or clue.

Instead, around a curve she sees the house, the *house* itself, rising out of a jungle of silver maple saplings, hundreds of them. The leaves flash and flutter in the breeze. A realtor's sign lies on its side in the tall grass near the stump of the big silver maple that had thrown its wide shade across the front lawn the summer of the reunion. And what Olivia feels as they wade and push through the thick grass and saplings toward the house is an emotion so quick and powerful it takes her by surprise. It's as potent as love *recovered*—the feeling itself, not the memory—an urge to laugh out loud and also a longing for no particular person or thing, a longing to *know* what the longing is for.

Olivia thinks that if the house had been sold and neglected—the screens kicked out, the yard full of junk cars—or if it had been salvaged—a picket fence thrown around it, a wreath of artificial flowers on the front door—its power to move her would have been lost in its new life. As it is, the power is original, strong. She feels as if she could look in and see them all eating dinner while Martha circles the long table, pouring raw milk into the children's glasses, and the mothers follow her, pouring it out and refilling the glasses with the store-bought, pasteurized kind.

Of course, what she sees when they've waded through the grass and stepped over the rotten place on the porch and looked in through the cloudy glass of the narrow window beside the door is the front room of an abandoned and neglected house. Bloated chairs, scattered papers, white bird droppings everywhere, a cardboard box packed with blue bottles. She *has* to get inside.

Down the mountain they find the realtor. Billie is her name. She has diamonds on the wings of her glasses, jewels on her long black T-shirt, ragged black hair and Cherokee-dark eyes, Cherokee cheekbones. She is so heavy and short of breath that Olivia's husband has to boost her up the broken front steps, but once they're inside the house, she turns brisk, businesslike. Martha's children still own the place, but they're so busy they never come here. That's why it's for sale. Someone is about to buy this place and turn it into a bed-and breakfast, take advantage of the business from the new ski slope over at Scaly Mountain. Since Olivia is kin (Billie can see the resemblance, yes: "You favor your aunt Martha," she says), wouldn't she be interested in buying it? Of course, Olivia would have to make an offer right away, today. Billie checks her watch. She's expecting an offer any minute from the bed and breakfast people.

Books lie scattered on the floor of every room; faded curtains droop from rusty rods; blackberry vines tap against the glass in the kitchen door. "You know, people around here say this place is haunted," Billie calls to Olivia as Olivia starts up the stairs to the second floor. "Your great-aunt Martha died in this house, and they say she came back as a cat to haunt it."

Olivia laughs. "If anyone would haunt a place, it would be Martha," she calls down the stairs, thinking of the grizzled tabby with the shredded ear that had been sitting on the porch when they drove up, and disappeared into the foundation like smoke when they stepped out of the car. Thinking of Martha's tenacity. The legendary struggle with her brother over the cream. She thinks of Martha fighting battles, righting wrongs, the clean, bleached smell of her clothes. There was no doubt about it—Martha wanted something out of life that couldn't be found in one lifetime. Naturally, her spirit would linger here, poking and probing and quarreling on, striding, big nose first, into a room.

Remembering all that, Olivia steps into the long room under the eaves where the women and girls slept during the reunion. Now it is full of rusty file cabinets and suitcases with busted hinges and, strangest of all, a wedding dress and veil, vacuum-packed in a long white box with a clear plastic window in the top. The windows are set so low in the wall she has to stoop to look through one of them. She sees her husband following their son through the tall grass behind the house, and beyond him, a dip in the overgrown meadow where Martha's pond once lay, that shallow, cold, muddy pond that never ran clear except where it flowed over the spillway.

Olivia opens a drawer in one of the file cabinets—she has to yank it because of the rust—and flips through crumbling file folders stuffed with brown and brittle papers. Real estate forms, a Rosicrucian newsletter, yellowed stationery with *Long Family Reunion* printed across the top. She thinks of the week she spent in this room, The Henhouse, the men had called it. All that clucking, fussing preening. A bunch of broody hens. Her father, who loved jokes, made a sign for the door. He lettered the name on a piece of cardboard, and underneath it he drew a plump hen with a big behind and long eyelashes looking coyly over her shoulder.

Olivia had never before been included among the women nor surrounded by so many of them. They slept under starched sheets and thin blankets in rows of rusty camp beds. She'd pulled her bed over near the window next to her mother's bed and the basket where her baby brother spent his one summer on earth. From that bed she watched the moon rise, the constellations wheel up from behind the mountain, the morning light fill the valley. The month before she died, so Olivia heard, Martha added a sunroom onto the south side of the house. And now this house and all its rooms have been left and locked away, abandoned, begun again and never finished.

"Your aunt Martha really knew her way around these mountains," Billie calls up from the bottom of the stairs. "One time she and a friend from out of town went to a neighbor's funeral at the Church of God up the road. The other woman dressed up in high heels, a nice navy dress, a mink stole, and a hat.

Well, those Church of God people are *strict,* you know. They don't allow any fancy show in their churches. They say that after that woman came in and took a seat, dressed in all her finery, everybody turned and stared her down until she left their church. But your aunt Martha now, she wore a plain black cardigan sweater over a dark dress. She wore low-heeled shoes. She came in and sat in a back pew, quiet and humble as a mouse, and they let her stay like she belonged there."

Olivia is pleased to hear a story about Martha's dignity for a change. Billie's story restores height and luster to the foolish and shopworn figure her aunt became in the stories that came down through the family. All over that part of the mountains, Billie says, people talked about Martha and that funeral.

5.

When the story got back to Martha that long ago fall, she hadn't seen what all the fuss was about. Dressing for the funeral that morning, she didn't give a thought to what she would wear: everyone knows what to wear to a *funeral.* She just reached into her closet and pulled out a black dress. Since it was a cool fall morning, she added a black sweater. At the last minute she even slipped off her wristwatch and left it in a dresser drawer to keep its gold band from offending the eye of any member of that stern congregation. The watch had been a birthday gift from her children one year, and looking at it reminded her of their faces—small and clear and full of light—when they were young and the days ahead seemed numberless.

She went into the crowded, chilly church and sat in the back pew and listened to the singing with her eyes closed. Harsh, unaccompanied, the sound reminded her of a dry creek bed, but that creek carried her anyway, back to the summer of the reunion and the walk she'd taken to the orchard with her grandchildren. The haunted orchard, the children called it, where a blight had killed the trees and withered apples still clung to the branches. Standing there with the children, she turned to her daughter's oldest boy. "And what do you intend to make of yourself when you grow up, young Mr. Albert?" she asked.

He looked up at her out of pale blue eyes and pivoted on his heels, inscribing circles in the dirt. He was ten, beginning to fizz. He wore red hightops, a whistle hanging from a lumpy purple-and-orange lanyard he'd made at Boy Scout camp earlier that summer. "A fifty-cent millionaire," he said, grinning.

Hearing Raymond's words in the child's mouth made her heart pound, her cheeks flush. And just like that, Raymond walked up and joined them. Uninvited, unwelcome, he came back with his gosh-and-golly face, his pale traitor's arm, all the things she'd made herself cold and deaf and blind to years ago. "Well, son-of-a-gun," she heard him whisper warmly in her ear, insinuating more. "How about them apples?"

"I hope you won't waste too much of your valuable time on that foolishness," she said to the boy. She stared at the orchard and felt suddenly dizzy, as though she'd felt the earth's circling, the endless motion of return that brought her here, where it seemed for a moment that the stubborn and contradictory truths of those trees merged with the warring truths of her own life: the trees had died, but the fruit would not fall. Hope could cling to nothing and a shriveled apple was all it took to bring love slinking back into this world. Inside the fruit she saw seeds; inside the seeds, more fruit. In this motion she saw the turning shadow that eternity throws across the world and also the current that carries us there.

At the funeral, when the hymn was done, the preacher told the story of the narrow gate, the strict accounting, the raked, leveled, and weeded ground of the promised land toward which they traveled in sure and certain hope of the resurrection. And when the service was over, she stood outside the church and greeted those harsh and unblinking souls as if they were kin.

ABOUT THE AUTHOR

PAM DURBAN is the author of the novels *The Laughing Place* (winner of the Townsend Prize), *So Far Back* (winner of the Lillian Smith Award), *The Tree of Forgetfulness,* and the short story collection *All Set About with Fever Trees.* Her short fiction has been published in *Georgia Review, Tri-Quarterly, Southern Review, Shenandoah, Crazyhorse, Epoch, New Virginia Review, Ohio Review,* and elsewhere. Durban has received a National Endowment for the Arts Creative Writing Fellowship and a Whiting Writer's Award as well as a James Michener Creative Writing Fellowship from the University of Iowa. With former Georgia poet laureate David Bottoms, she is founding coeditor of *Five Points* literary magazine. A native of Aiken, South Carolina, she is the Doris Betts Distinguished Professor of Creative Writing at the University of North Carolina at Chapel Hill.